So Close to Heaven

A Novel

ANNETTE OPPENLANDER

First published by Annette Oppenlander, 2023
First Edition
annetteoppenlander.com
Averesch 93, 48683 Ahaus, Germany
Text Copyright: Annette Oppenlander 2023
ISBN: 978-3-948100-38-4 eBook
ISBN: 978-3-948100-39-1 Paperback

Editing: Cecily Blench, The History Quill
Design: http://www.fiverr.com/akira007

DEDICATION

Throughout history, thousands if not tens of thousands of women have contributed to the wellbeing of others and to the achievements of mankind. Many of those women remain nameless and forgotten. Let them be remembered and cherished.

Other Books by Annette Oppenlander

English
A Different Truth (Historical Mystery, Vietnam War Era)
Escape From the Past Trilogy (Time-travel Adventure)
47 Days: How Two Teen Boys Defied the Third Reich
(Novelette)
Everything We Lose: A Civil War Novel of Hope, Courage
and Redemption
Surviving the Fatherland (WWII Biographical Novel)
Where the Night Never Ends: A Prohibition Era Novel
When They Made Us Leave (WWII Historical Novel)
A Lightness in My Soul: Inspired by a True Story (WWII
Novella)
The Scent of a Storm (WWII Historical Novel)

German
Vaterland, wo bist Du? Roman nach einer wahren Geschichte
Erzwungene Wege: Historischer Roman
47 Tage (Novelle)
Immer der Fremdling: Die Rache des Grafen
Bis uns nichts mehr bleibt (Amerikanischer Bürgerkrieg)
Erfolgreich(e) historische Romane schreiben: Wie man Leser
in die Vergangenheit entführt
Leicht wie meine Seele (Novelle)
Als Deutschlands Jungen ihre Jugend verloren
Endlos ist die Nacht

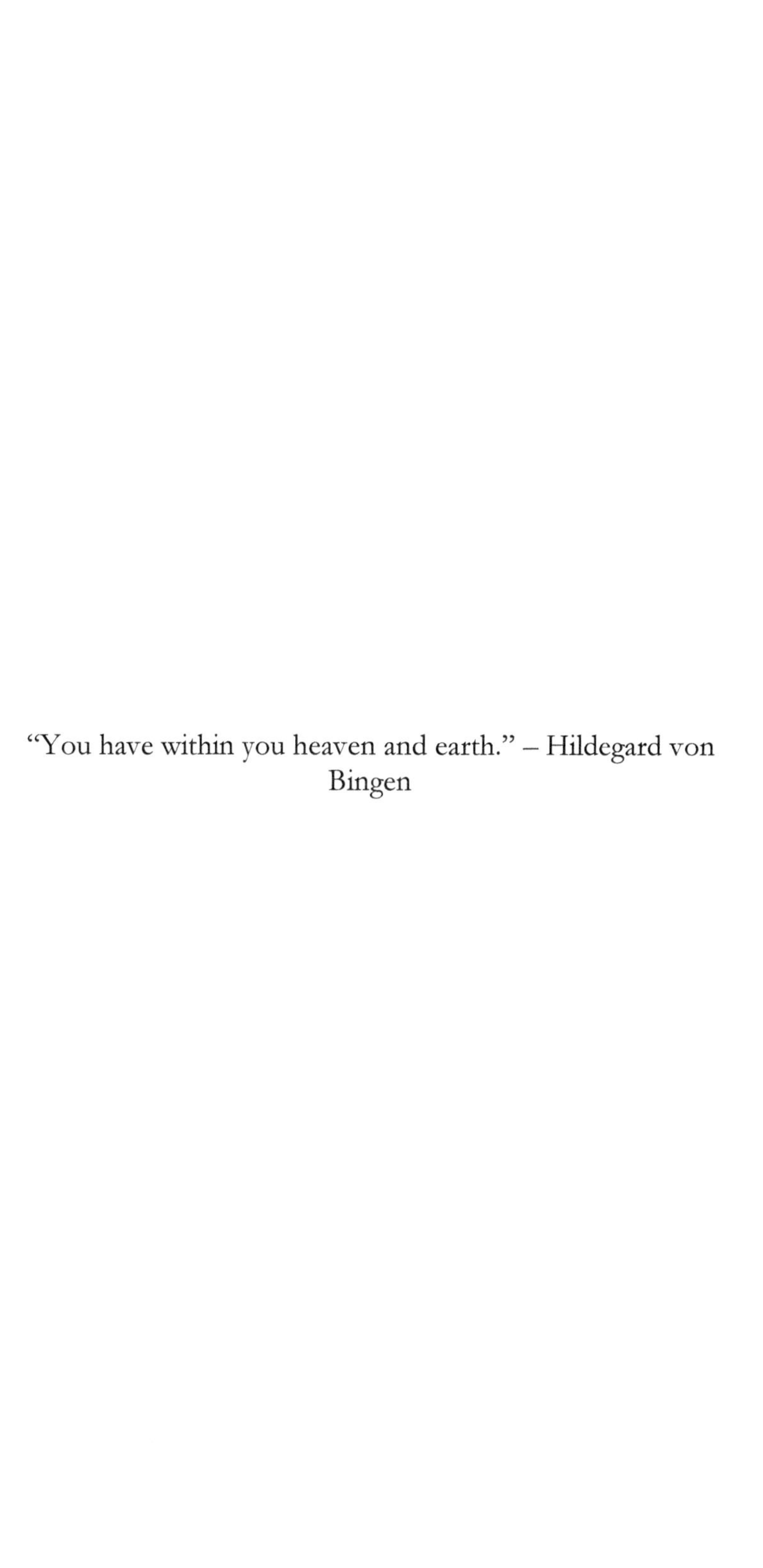

"You have within you heaven and earth." – Hildegard von Bingen

Inspired by a True Story

PROLOGUE

/Sin/: An immoral act considered to be a transgression against divine law.

The girl's long dark hair clings to her face and back. Rain hammers the ground with such intensity, the drops jump up as if possessed. The sound of rushing water fills the air, brooks and rivulets gurgle and splash on their race to the valley. It is dark, so dark, the girl picks her steps carefully, like a blind person on an unknown road. Yet she knows these hills, these paths, the breathtaking vistas of these alpine pastures. Knows them like only somebody who has grown up here can.

Somewhere in the distance, lightning flashes, illuminates a sheer rock wall rising into the heavens, the stunted gnarly trees below like stubby black arms. The air is cold up here, much colder than in the valley where the girl came from. She is not dressed for this, the fabric of her skirt heavy with water, her blouse and bodice too thin to keep out the wind. She wears no coat, no bag or pack, not even decent shoes.

Yet the girl does not seem to notice. She walks slowly, dreamlike, yet with purpose. It is the place she left that gives her this purpose. It is spring, April, a month when nature up here still pivots between winter and summer. Snow clings to the tops, and the rain is not far from freezing. In good weather, these peaks kiss the sky, a sky that takes on a blue as deep as the Caribbean Sea, so clear, it almost scorches the eyes.

At dawn, the girl slows and finally sinks onto a boulder. She squeezes out her hair, hugs herself as white clouds rise from her lips. Her gaze travels in the direction she came from as if she is expecting an attack. She is a pretty thing, her eyes the warm brown of chestnuts, her mouth generous, though with a stubborn streak. The chestnut brown repeats in her hair, the rich earthy color of a beautiful fall day. A scratch, now crusted over, crosses her right cheek. It is deep and must hurt, but there is no pain in the girl's features, just apprehension.

When a deer breaks from the forest, she jumps to her feet and continues down the path. Below her in the mist lies another village, one of many that squeeze in between the mountains of northern Italy, a region they call South Tirol.

But the girl does not head downward, she makes her way along the mountain path, her feet sure despite her unfit shoes, the slippery rocks and gravel. Her pauses grow longer and more frequent. She is exhausted. At some point, she drinks from one of the frequent brooks that rush across her path, then takes off her shoes and massages her feet. She is slender, not bony, her body that of a fully developed woman, her hips slim with small breasts beneath the bodice made of green linen.

By noon, she begins to struggle. The sun pokes weakly through the clouds, illuminating the first wildflowers on the meadows that sweep hundreds of feet across the hills. Up here, the sky continues forever, a blue and white canopy of infinity.

She finally stops. Again, her eyes wander to the path she has come along, then turn again the other way. Uncertainty plays on her features now, her chin trembles.

At some point, the girl begins to climb again—on and up, across the next mountaintop. It is midafternoon now and her pace is sluggish. Yet she does not stop any longer, she continues past the villages below her, whose red clay roofs reflect the last sun. Soon, they disappear in the shadow of the mountains once more.

Sheep bleat somewhere, a forlorn sound that travels along the sheer cliffs. The girl approaches a tiny cabin, no more than ten by ten feet of rough-hewn larch with a stone fireplace. In the fading light, she slips inside, skims the few pots and containers for nourishment. Unable to find any, she bends before the fire pit and lights kindling with a flint. She rubs herself as the flame takes and sends out the first warmth.

In a corner, the girl discovers a moth-eaten sheepskin. She wraps herself in it and curls up before the fire, falls asleep like only the exhausted can.

Somewhere outside, five or six kilometers to the east, three men carry torches. They shout, "Mariele, Mariele, where are you?"

The girl does not hear them. She is sleeping without dreams as her limbs reclaim some of the warmth.

Sometime in the early hours, she jerks awake. She does not know why, only senses that something is wrong. Dread creeps up her back like the tentacles of an octopus. She straightens and wraps the sheepskin around her shoulders… listens. Outside, a thin moon throws deep shadows across ragged peaks. Inside, the fire is out.

Voices, nearly imperceptible, reach the cabin, impossible to determine where they come from. A jolt travels through the girl, takes hold of her slender frame until she trembles from head to toe. She rushes to the door, carefully opens it and listens. It is too dark to see much, a heavy mist lies across the meadows. The icy air crawls beneath her skin, deeper yet into her bones. She shivers more violently, but all she does is listen.

The voices grow louder. "She could not have come this far, not in this weather. She has no coat… wears her good shoes."

"I do not know why she would run away like that," announces another voice. "It makes no sense. She has always been sensible." This man's voice is quieter than the others, older, yet reaches her easily. It is this voice the girl fears most, wishes it to go away.

"Let us hurry. Some place around here is a sheepherder's hut. Maybe she is waiting for morning to return to us…"

The girl creeps outside. The voices are close now, so close they'll see her any moment. Quickly, she ducks low and sneaks around back. There is an overhang to store wood. A small space, no more than two feet across, opens behind it. The girl climbs into the hole and drapes the sheepskin she is still clutching over her head.

On the other side, voices grow loud now… animated. "Here it is. I knew it was close." It is the voice of the older man. Triumph swings in it, but also something else, something dark and menacing.

"Nobody in here," the second voice says. "The fireplace is still warm, though."

"She must have been here. I just know it."

"Maybe we should wait and search in daylight."

"Nonsense, we cannot wait. It is dangerous, she may fall to her death."

The older man scoffs. "She knows these peaks like mountain goats. I have taken her many times to visit other villages. We will just miss her in the dark."

"All right, then. It is only a couple of hours till dawn, let us take a break."

"What about a guard?"

"You are guarding against what? Mariele's attack?" Rough laughter follows.

"Never mind, we rest now."

Outside, the girl cautiously climbs from her hiding spot and straightens. She is cold, colder than she has ever been in her life, but despite her bluish lips and stiff knees, she tiptoes into the darkness. Only when she is around the next bend does she speed up her steps. It is delicate work on the loose ground, but she welcomes this task to distract her from her pursuers. Rocks slide away, some roll over the edge, and, after what seems like an eternity, land some place far below—a false step will end it all.

The girl keeps her gaze on the path and the precipice to her right, her mouth is set as she walks away from the men to put distance between her and them.

At dawn, she halts briefly, throws an anxious glance over her shoulder. Across from her, across a narrow valley sit walled buildings and several churches. The girl's eyes are fixed on them as the first rays of the sun sparkle on their roofs. A bell rings like a call, a metallic yet melodic sound that travels with ease across the expanse.

The trembling in the girl's shoulders stops. She continues to gaze at the abbey perched like an eagle's nest on the rock, hundreds of feet above the Eisack valley. A different expression moves into her eyes, one of hope. If she could fly, she would be there in minutes.

Then she sets her mouth as something new takes over her features: resolve.

PART I
CHAPTER ONE

Sabiona Abbey, South Tirol, July 1796

I am sorting through my collection of tomato and pepper seeds in the greenhouse when Sister Adelheid rushes through the door. Her round face – everything on her is round, even her hands – is flushed as she cries, "Sister Magdalena, come quick. The Abbess needs you."

I tuck my beloved seeds back into their box and follow Sister Adelheid uphill. She is huffing for air because the slope to the main house is steep. I am lucky to be used to it from my daily ministrations in the garden.

"What happened?" I ask, but Adelheid just raises her arms, and the wind, which is brisk most times up here, makes her habit flutter and reminds me of the wings of a crow. She is quiet, even for a nun, and I quit pressuring. Even now, after all these years, the sin of impatience is difficult to master.

Abbess Mayrin already waits in the entrance to the main house along with the hulking figure of Chaplain Father Schweiggl. We may be a Benedictine abbey of nuns, but Father Schweiggl serves as our confessor. He dismisses Adelheid with a nod and waves me and Abbess Mayrin along.

"We must pray, Sister Magdalena, for strength and

wisdom." Abbess Mayrin's usually calm voice is strained and I recognize distress between her scrunched brows. They are thick and dark with speckles of gray like those of a man, but vanity is not something we subscribe to at the abbey.

Father Schweiggl remains silent, only flings up his hood to cover his shaven head.

Voices rear from beyond the walls, a lot of voices—the voices of men. How could I not have heard them earlier?

"The Tirolean army," the Abbess huffs at the same time. "Sister Augusta says they are a hundred seventy fighters."

Augusta is our gate sister. She was born with a clubfoot and has been here for half a century.

"What do they want?" I ask. My breath is no longer calm, and I tuck at the wimple that surrounds my face.

Father Schweiggl grumbles, "We will know in a moment."

Sister Augusta fidgets when she sees us. Her eyes are wide with worry, her cheeks on fire as she limps toward us. "They will not listen," she says. "It cannot be."

Abbess Mayrin catches Augusta's hands and holds them. "What cannot be?"

"They demand entry." From the sister's lips, it sounds as if the men plan on flying like birds.

"But why?" says the Abbess. I am thankful for her calmness, yet I detect apprehension, which in turn makes me worry even more. I take a deep breath, straighten my shoulders—I must be strong.

Augusta's eyes shimmer with tears. She is probably over seventy and has trouble standing. "They want to live here."

Schweiggl lifts a calming hand. "Let me talk to them."

Together we step to the gate, where men in traditional work attire and heavy beards crowd the path. There are so many, they snake along the towering walls around the curve and out of sight. Many of them carry muskets, some picks. All look as if they are ready to devour us.

I send up a prayer for strength and courage. They must

not see my fear, my trembling knees well hidden beneath the tunic.

"Beg your pardon," a fresh-faced man says, leaning his musket against the side of the gate. He cannot be older than twenty, with hair the color of copper, a long curved nose and high cheekbones. "I am Joachim Haspinger. We must request entry. Our men require quarters to prepare for the French army."

"On what orders?" Schweiggl says.

"Do you have papers?" Abbess Mayrin's right eye is twitching as she kneads the wooden cross between her fingers.

The young man whips out a wrinkled sheet with a seal that is broken, the paper red-stained where the wax once was.

Schweiggl and Abbess Mayrin read it while I try to catch a glimpse…

Below a massive crest with a red and gold crown and a red lion are a few lines: *by decree of the emperor, Franz II… immediate support… unconditional.* The paper quivers in Abbess Mayrin's hand and her face is nearly as white as her coif.

"You are to give us shelter," the young man says. He hesitates. "Surely you have heard of General Bonaparte… the war?"

Of course, we have heard shreds of news. Word is slow to travel up here, our abbey only reachable on foot, but we know that Napoleon Bonaparte has invaded Italy and won most battles. He appears hungry to conquer what is not his.

"How long?" breaks from my lips as my thoughts gallop to Benedict's teachings. Guests are supposed to be welcomed and fed. My heart cringes as I listen to the mumbles of the men crowding the gate. Some smile, some are looking angry, others tired. *You are a Benedictine nun,* my mind cries. *Act like one.*

But these are no pilgrims. How can I welcome guests when they show up like wild animals ready to devour our abbey—our home?

"We do not know. We will be fighting the French when they get here," the young man says. "Most of us are from the area, but we need a place to train and hide."

"We require time to prepare," the Abbess says resolutely.

"No need," the man says. "We will be happy to situate ourselves."

"Surely we can come to an agreement." Schweiggl tries a smile, but the young man ignores it.

He simply steps forward and walks past the open-mouthed Abbess. I pull her aside before the mob can run us down. Like a broken dam, the men march past us, the air thick with the stench of unwashed bodies and lurking gazes.

Until my attention is drawn to an older man who carries a well-oiled musket. He is tall and muscular and must be close to my age. Only there is something in his expression that I recognize, the heavy brows, the sneer that makes him appear equally dangerous and calculating.

My knees, then my ankles grow soft. I want to turn away, want to run, but all I do is step backward to lean against the wall next to Sister Augusta, who fans herself.

"What a shame, how can they do that?" she says, but I am unable to look at her or speak a single word. The man has moved up with the crowd and almost reached us. The scar cutting across his forehead and losing itself in the hairline is clearly visible. There is no more doubt, I know this man. All of a sudden, I feel dirty.

Lower your head, my mind shouts. Ever so slowly, my body follows and I look down, so the veil shades my face. My chest constricts as I envision the man gripping my arm, tearing away my habit. It cannot be, he is dead. It has to be my imagination.

The banging of the closing gate pulls me back to the present. Sister Augusta sinks onto her stool. "It is a terrible hardship for the abbey," she says, misunderstanding what must surely be written on my features—panic.

"Quick, we must tell the others," Abbess Mayrin says to me. I completely forgot she was there. "How will we feed them?"

I force my mind to the same subject. Our stores in the cellars are full, a fact I am proud of. As cellarin, I am responsible for the nourishment of our convent.

Our abbey is large, but one hundred seventy hungry men? They will not only eat us out of everything, they will drink our wine. All of it. We do not indulge, Benedict is clear about us living with a minimum only, but we do use wine for mass.

By the time we walk toward the main house, cries and shrieks ring out through the open windows. It is a beautiful July day and most of the sisters are airing their cells. I feel for them, and yet my mind is on the man who is now within these walls. Has he recognized me?

Deep voices reverberate from the walls, walls that have never seen such mayhem. Off and on, we host priests or pilgrims. Benedict says we are to pray with our guests, help support them in their belief in God. The Abbess is supposed to spray water over their hands, wash their feet.

It is impossible, oh, God. I want to kneel right here and pray, but there is no time. I must help my fellow sisters grapple with this strange new world.

It turns out the men do not want our help. They just trample across our holy corridors, break our silence. Some have made it into the cellar and by the time I get there, the iron gate's lock is broken, kegs are opened. Some men are drinking by lifting the wine to their beard-covered lips, blessed wine saved for mass. Another has found the brandy we keep for ailments of the stomach and mouth. My heart bleeds as I stand there, my key no longer needed.

"Sister, where is your kitchen?" a fellow with long unkempt locks asks. He is carrying one of the air-dried hams we serve during Sunday *Vespers*. Another with a terrible limp and a scar across his cheek grins at me, revealing brownish stumps of teeth.

I cringe. *Lixivum dentale* goes through my head, wishing to prescribe my favorite teeth cleaning remedy, Hildegard von Bingen's vine ash wine… vines cut in spring… burn only the cleanest to make ash… Hildegard is my favorite Benedictine abbess. Even though she lived more than six hundred years ago, she was not only smart and well read, she was a healer and assembled the most amazing medicines. Many of our sisters are benefiting from the herbs I am growing next to our vegetables and fruits.

I do not even want to know the state of my beloved gardens.

"Well, where is it then?" The fellow with the messy locks watches me intently. Down here in the gloom of the cellars, his eyes appear black as coal chutes.

Somewhere above me, a cry rings out. It is so dreadful, I move toward it without answering the man. He does not seem to care because he follows me, along with several others. I rush upstairs, glad I am healthy, glad I can lead the way in front of these intruders. They will destroy our kitchens—my pride and joy.

You are not to feel pride, the voice in my head comments. *You are here to serve God.* I must work on my sins, pray for forgiveness, but right now, I must help my sisters.

CHAPTER TWO

Upon entering the kitchen, I discover Sister Gertrud lying prostrate on the prep counter near the sink. Two men have pushed her down, one attempting to clamp a hand across her mouth to keep her from shrieking.

"What is the meaning of this?" I shout.

The two men fumble to straighten, their eyes still shiny with lust. Sister Gertrud is our newest novice and she is pretty in a worldly way, with a well-shaped mouth and the sapphire eyes of Lake Kalterer. Right now, they are opaque with fear and she scrambles off in a hurry.

Behind me, the men from the basement have entered. I feel their presence, smell their stench. Where is the man with the scar across his forehead? *I am not afraid.*

"I must insist that you leave us alone," I say, proud that my voice does not betray me.

"Says who?" one of the hooligans mocks. The broad nose, which looks like it was broken more than once, and his dull expression, make him look dimwitted. The eyes do not help. They are small and mean and reddened like a wild boar's.

"We shall do what we please," his cohort says.

I put on what I hope is a steely expression. "I demand to see your leader."

"He is busy elsewhere," says the man with the broken

nose. "What are you going to do about it?"

What indeed? I am unaccustomed to such treatment, such rawness. I have long forgotten what it means to deal with common men. The few monks and pilgrims finding us here on this remote mountain are always quiet and polite guests and Father Schweiggl keeps to himself most of the time. I stand there as the soldiers behind me crowd closer. A shove sends me forward toward the table. What will I do if they… I am nearly forty-two years old. I want to pray to God for wisdom, but my brain is hollow, a pit of inky air. I forget where I am, watch the men lick their lips. I remember those looks, the shiny eyes, the grins. I must not—

"What is going on here?" The young man, Haspinger, who spoke at the gate earlier pushes through the crowd and places himself between the two men and me near the table. He is still carrying the musket, but now I also see a well-cared for knife on his hip. He is tall, almost six feet, and towers over most of the others.

Mumbles rise in the room, nothing I understand, but I can tell they are disappointed to miss a spectacle… or maybe a turn for themselves.

I clear my throat. "I found your men tormenting one of our novices."

"Is that true?" Haspinger's gaze travels around the room until he locks eyes with the man with the piggish face. "You part of it?"

The mean eyes turn toward the ground.

"Make yourself useful, fetch water. And you." His gaze lands on the other thug. "Start a fire."

Obviously, this is not the first time these two have made trouble. And obviously, despite his youth, the men respect Haspinger.

Now he turns to me. "I am very sorry, Sister. I will have a word with the men." He bows and begins to shout orders to the others and soon everybody is too busy to pay attention to me.

For the first time since I became cellarin, I feel useless.

My afternoon prayer has come and gone. It cannot be helped. I must find the Abbess, because now that the men have taken over the kitchen, an idea forms in my head.

Outside, I hear nuns cry out. Like the men, it is a foreign sound; even with dozens of sisters, it is always quiet. We talk a little when we work or spend time together, pray and sing.

My feet carry me uphill to the highest point of Sabiona. I almost stumble up the steps to the heavy wooden doors, step through and… am alone. The Church of the Holy Cross is my favorite of Sabiona Abbey's four churches.

It is small and less ornate than the abbey's main church. I kneel in front of the sculpture of Mary Magdalene, bow my head. I was named after her in a holy ceremony many years ago.

"Give me strength and wisdom," I murmur. "I beg you to show me the path." *Do not let him see me.*

I listen for her words, sink deeper into the silence. Mary Magdalene has been a complicated figure, considered unworthy by some because she was a prostitute. But are we not all sinners, carrying secrets about things we did or that happened to us that we are not proud of? Mary Magdalene repented and was the first to witness Jesus's rise. I must remember her feast day on July 22.

What day is it? My brain spins away.

Over the years, I have developed a sense of quiet within these walls. I can sit still for hours… contemplate, think and pray. In here, I feel safe and removed from the world as if existing in a cocoon. The air smells of incense with a slight musty note, and remains cool, no matter what the temperature is outside.

Of course, I do not have much time as we pray six times a day and I am charged with the organization of the kitchen and our stocks.

My mind races back to the mayhem in the cellars, the scene in the kitchen… the man who tormented me many years ago and has infiltrated these walls. My chest constricts, my hand wanders to my neck, tugs at the coif. I feel trapped, the abbey's walls that protected me now hold danger.

The opening door behind me pulls me from my thoughts.

I must speak to the Abbess.

I find Abbess Mayrin pacing the hall in front of her quarters.

"I have got an idea," I cry as soon as I draw near. Above us, footsteps clatter, some heavy and aggressive, others lighter and fleeting. "We could move into the guest quarters. It will be cramped, but it is at least away from the main house. We cannot tolerate men on our floors, even if there were enough cells."

Abbess Mayrin stops pacing and faces me. "We should speak to Father Schweiggl."

I bite back a comment. He cannot help us, not now. I do not want Schweiggl so close, certainly not living amongst us. "Maybe Father Schweiggl can stay with the other men… keep an eye on them?"

"That may be a good idea," Abbess Mayrin says. "What about the kitchen?" She is always calm, but right now, she squeezes the cross dangling from the beaded necklace.

I shake my head. "They are using it. We will make do with the guest kitchen." It will be a challenge, our cooking vessels are small and will not hold enough food for dozens of nuns.

Abbess Mayrin sighs. "All right then, tell the sisters. I will find Schweiggl and this Habinger… Haspinger."

I hurry upstairs, stick my head into each cell, alert my family. "To the guesthouse, grab your things." At the same time, I watch for the man with the scar. All I can hope is that he will not recognize me.

In front of some rooms, habits, shoes, bibles and underthings are piled up in heaps. Some soldiers have moved in without waiting.

In an alcove, I find Sister Gertrud kneeling on the floor, her habit a black cloud.

"I cannot bear it," she cries as I take her elbow to help her up. Her usually luminous eyes are clouded, her skin puffy. "I have been praying for enlightenment, but God does not answer. Why would he send us such men?"

Why indeed? But aloud I say, "Maybe he is testing us. They are supposed to defend the country."

"I know I have sinned," she quickly crosses herself, "but this is a terrible test."

"Come now, I will go with you. We are moving into the guesthouse."

By the time everybody is situated—most sisters have to share rooms—I have missed two more prayer times. Haspinger has agreed to keep his men away from us. For the time being, quiet has settled. It should calm me, but I am not calm. I must feed our community and I do not think our food will last more than a week or two. Normally, we supplement many meals from our garden, but it is not built for hundreds of people.

To distract myself, I hurry outside. My raspberry vines have been trampled, their fruit taken by the men. They have not touched my cauliflowers, tomatoes or peppers, but it is a matter of time. We must send word to Klausen, the village at the foot of the mountain, where we order our supplies.

I sink to my knees to pull weeds in the tiny flower patch, touching the soil soothes me. The little rose bush is blooming in a profusion of red and I remove spent buds.

"Sister Magdalena?"

I startle at the sound, try to remain calm and not let him see my fear. It is the man with the scar, Georg Teiner. I remain bent over the rose, hope my voice is calm. "Yes?"

"Commander Haspinger is asking for you." Outwardly, Georg sounds calm, but I know better. Back in the day, his mood would switch from detached to explosive in a second.

"I will go in a minute," I mumble.

"I am supposed to take you to him."

I consider smearing dirt all over my face, grimace at my

silliness. Instead, I straighten, which thankfully is still pretty easy. I keep my head lowered, intent on following behind him.

But as soon as we walk off, he moves next to me. I can feel his curious stare like a branding iron on my temple.

Nobody is on the path, nobody to distract him or help me.

"You look familiar, do I know you?"

I keep my head low, hurry uphill. Faster. I must not be alone with this man.

"Wait!" Fingers grab a fistful of my sleeve, bring me to a stop.

I try to pull away, the grip holds. Normal people do not touch a nun—

"Mariele?" Georg now towers in front of me, cuts off my escape route. He finds my wrist, squeezes like an iron cuff. "It *is* you." He shakes his head. "I… we thought you were dead, had fallen to your death in some crevasse. All these years." His voice sounds low and composed, but I know better. "Damn, do you have any idea how worried we were for you? And here you are, playing nun." He spits.

I say nothing. Cannot. All the fear has returned. I do not even have the strength to lift my head.

"Say something. Why, Mariele?"

"Sister Magdalena."

"Bullshit!" He roughly pushes my chin upward, so that I am forced to look at him.

"I must go—"

"Why?" He spits again, still stares at me. One of the sisters once said the soul of a person reflects in their eyes. If that is true, Georg's must be buried beneath a frozen lake.

"Why did you leave and hide here?"

Do you really have to ask?

"Speak to me, it is the least I deserve."

You deserve nothing, I want to scream. Instead, I try to step backwards.

"Not so fast." A bitter chuckle escapes Georg as he squeezes my wrist. "You almost killed me, made me the laughingstock of Niederdorf, the entire valley. I could not show my face without people talking."

Alarm bells ring in my head. "I must go." Again I pull, again he resists. I consider kicking him, but my tunic is in the way.

"Teiner, did you find the sister? Haspinger is waiting." A young man with a green felt hat has come to a stop next to us.

"I am ready to see your commander," I say quickly while yanking my arm free.

The young man nods. "Come with me."

"This is not over." Rage distorts Georg's voice. "You owe me."

I hurry after the young man as my heart bangs against my ribs. A weight sits on my chest and I gasp for breath.

The young man throws me a worried glance. "I am sorry, Sister, I walk too fast."

All I want to do is hug him for saving me.

CHAPTER THREE

That night, I do not sleep much in my new cell. Benedict tells us to be obedient, live in harmony in our community, and without material possessions. Indeed, my move into the guesthouse has been swift with just a spare habit, a few underthings and my winter shoes. I also have a bible and Hildegard von Bingen's book, *Physica*. It is sinful to covet books, but it is one of the few things the Abbess allows.

My thoughts are returning to the encounter with Georg. He reminds me of a powder keg, ready to explode at the slightest provocation. I want to disappear, want to remain hidden in here forever.

My new cell is smaller, but basically the same, a bed, a chair, a washbasin and a cross. It is a smaller Jesus here, but he looks just as mournful. I sit in darkness and even though I have no clock, I know it will be time for first prayer soon.

I should not covet things, but I miss my old room.

It was just as bare, and yet? Somehow the walls I spent every night in for the past twenty-three years are familiar. They have soaked up my thoughts, listened to them, given me comfort when I felt troubled. It is the quality of the air inside, a calmness I crave that comforts my soul. It is a cocoon of sorts, almost like a womb, away from the world, safe—even more removed than the abbey, clinging to the highest rock above Klausen. They call it Mount Sabiona or Holy Mountain. Indeed, up here, one can feel closer to God. Until now.

I wash with cold water, do not feel a thing. All I see is Georg's angry expression that barely hides the icy soul inside. Should I speak with Haspinger? And say what? To leave me alone and forget what happened? I cannot possibly share any of it.

In church, Sister Gertrud is already in front and, after a short prayer, she begins to recite a reading from the Old Testament. We sing our responsorium and after a moment of collection, we silently file outside.

The Abbess waits for me. "I have a letter for Bishop Lodron in Brixen. I am asking him to send help, appeal to the emperor."

"I will take it," I say. Usually, I would send one of the younger novices to the village, but I have decided to go myself, anything to get me away for a bit. Of course, there is no telling who may lurk in the bushes. But at least I will be away from Georg for an hour or two.

The village sends a runner once a week, but that is in another five days. We cannot wait that long.

Abbess Mayrin grips my hands. "Be careful, go with God."

I nod grimly.

As I hurry to the gate, snoring rises from some of the open windows in the main house. For a moment, I am disoriented, taken back to the inn my father ran in Niederdorf.

The Black Eagle often hosted travelers overnight, mostly merchants and pilgrims. My steps slow as the face of my father returns. It is clear for once, the unyielding mouth hidden by a full beard, the burning eyes. Only his voice never comes to me, though its memory is burned into my mind like the markings on a steer—never loud, yet sharp and dominant. Nobody risked angering my father. Only I…

Whispering voices bring me back. Near the entry and positioned along the outer wall stand guards. Haspinger must have placed them there to look out for Bonaparte's men. I imagine Georg among them, imagine him following me downhill.

Dutifully I lower my head and explain my errand. The soldier nods, his face hardly recognizable under the wilderness of his beard.

Despite the steepness of the path, I walk quickly. My thighs and knees complain a bit, but the air this morning is glorious—God's air—full of lavender and honeysuckle. I should not feel this happy to leave my home and part of me longs to be back in that all-knowing room, but the other part of me rejoices. It is still cool and a bit damp, but this will be another summer day.

The village of Klausen, at the foot of Sabiona Abbey, is a small town with narrow paths that straddles the Tinnebach, a creek full of the most amazing red boulders. In spring, the creek turns into angry, noisy white water. I drop my letter at the postal service and continue to the townhall. I must speak with the city's mayor, ask for advice.

I am back out in less than five minutes. The mayor is traveling, and his assistant shook his head and simply said there was no point. We need the Tirolean army to protect us. And where better to house them than in a monastery with plenty of space?

The only thing he did agree to was to give me a note for the merchants to send up supplies for the men… and sisters. I visit each of them, the baker, a vintner, and a few farmers nearby. All of them promise to help and send provisions by the weekend.

The hike back is not nearly as pleasant.

What is pleasant? I have no right to enjoy, I am here to serve God and if he has found it important to test us by sending these soldiers, I will do my best to work through it.

Back behind the walls of the abbey, dread returns. My earlier excitement and commitment to make the best of the situation are evaporating as I take inventory. Some of the men are lounging in our gardens, some smoke, others whittle or clean their muskets. In the courtyard, they practice marching and combat.

I used to walk with a straight back to enjoy the views over the valleys. Now I cower and look down, wishing for my veil to be longer.

The cellar is mostly empty. It is as if the soldiers have consumed everything overnight. The main kitchen is filthy, pots and plates are piled on all surfaces, kitchen waste, which I always compost for my garden, rots in a corner. Flies swarm above everything.

My beloved garden beds are trampled, two men are ripping onions from the soil.

Instead of asking them to stop—I remember what happened in the kitchen yesterday—I speed off in search of the leader, Haspinger. How is one so young already in charge?

The bell rings—prayer time. Haspinger has to wait. It is one of Benedict's rules that we interrupt whatever we do to pray—every three hours during the day. One might consider it difficult, but the regular prayer becomes its own pattern. It is comforting to return to God, be reminded that he is with us.

I turn toward the guesthouse, rinse my hands and join my sisters in church. But my concentration is less than perfect. The calm that usually descends inside this space and inside me is absent today. Some of the sisters sigh, some twitch. During prayer, their eyes rise up urgently. What would Mary Magdalene do? Surely, she must have dealt with difficult situations… men.

But there is no time to return to my cell and contemplate. Not today. After reporting to the Abbess, I find Haspinger in the midst of a group of soldiers, sitting in the sun. Immediately, I scan every face. The man… Georg… is not there. Haspinger is chewing a blade of grass, talking animatedly. Only when I approach and his gaze lands on me does he stop.

"I need to have a word," I say with my strong voice. It is a voice I hardly recognize, because we speak softly in our Benedictine sisterly community, *stabilitas*, our lifelong connection inside the abbey.

Being direct must work better than appearing too demure because Haspinger gets up and follows me to a quiet spot near an apple tree.

"As you know, I am in charge of the kitchen and cellars. We have got to discuss our supply situation." Haspinger nods but remains quiet, something I appreciate. "Our stores are nearly depleted, your men just help themselves. I did ask for deliveries, but they will not arrive until the weekend. And after that… We cannot feed everyone, the sisters—"

"It may be better if you all left."

Too stunned to speak, I just stare at the man. He might as well have said for us to plunge ourselves off the mountain.

"It is our home."

Haspinger shrugs and spits out the grass. "War does not care about people's homes." He frowns, but then he tries for a half smile. "Look, Sister… Magdalena, I appreciate your concern, but we need a place to stay and you have got the room. It is a strategic position, too important to ignore. The French will not care. They would be a good deal worse."

I swallow, try to grapple with this information, the new truth of our existence. Everything I took for granted has been shaken. Again.

I lower my head because I do not want the man to see my tears. I must stay strong now. Clearing my throat, I ask, "Will you organize additional supplies? Surely you will need to plan ahead… in case of a siege?"

"It is being done as we speak. We have got hunters, and other villages will deliver."

"I just ask that you do not forget about us…" *While we are here*, but I cannot make myself say it out loud.

"I will try." Haspinger hesitates. "You must understand that these men are not used to living… holy… they know women in taverns, their own families, most of them are farmers. They are getting ready to fight a war. It would be better if they were not tempted."

The lump in my throat threatens to take my air. The words hardly make it across my lips. "I will speak with Abbess Mayrin."

Haspinger abruptly tips his hat and returns to his men, while I fold my hands and lower my head to hide my desperation.

"We are supposed to do what?" Abbess Mayrin's eyes fill with tears just like mine earlier. "Where would we go? It is our home, our community."

I nod. I have no answers, not even ideas. Benedict's teachings state to remain together except for brief educational journeys. Each abbey, each monastery forms a tight community.

Abbess Mayrin presses her lips together and looks toward the ceiling. "God will guide us and only he will tell."

Again, I nod. I should mention Georg to the Abbess, but my throat is tight and sore. All I can hope is for the French to arrive and take him away. Oh, what am I thinking?

I have been so sure that God is always there to keep us, embrace us, protect us against evil. I realize it is easy to believe when one has little contact with humanity. Now humanity has invaded our realm.

What will God decide about that?

CHAPTER FOUR

Winter 1796–1797

I have never been this cold. Our guesthouse is not set up for the many nuns, the hearth in the kitchen smokes. Our cells do not have ovens and I dread each night. The blanket appears to be covered in ice and my bed remains nearly as frigid as the outside. My feet refuse to warm, no matter the socks I wear. It is worse for the older nuns.

I pray to forget the cold as we huddle in church. Some of the sisters have developed ailments of the chest. Sister Augusta is in bed with bronchitis. I have rubbed her chest and throat with oil of wormwood, Hildegard von Bingen's recipe for ailments of the lungs. Still, I worry she may not see spring.

But worse is the hunger. We are used to fasting, used to following Benedict's teachings of an ascetic life. He says we should avoid immoderacy, eating or drinking too much. There is no fear of that now. Thanks to the few well-meaning farmers, we have grain and still bake bread every morning, but meat is only served on Sundays now and most of our vegetable stores have disappeared. The potatoes I store for the winter are long gone. There is neither milk nor butter. The men devour it all, which forces us to hide our meager supplies.

But worst for me is the stench that has taken over our beloved abbey, even now when temperatures many times are at freezing or below. Our outhouses cannot service that many people. The sisters and I resort to using night pots and dumping them into a hole that Sister Gertrud and our newest novice, Sister Dorothea, dug at the lowest point of the grounds. Every day, we all make our way there to empty and rinse our pots.

But the men, oh, what brutes they are. Though I do not dare go near the outhouses, I smell them from afar. Worse is that the men relieve themselves anywhere they stand. It does not just reek and infect our most sacred places of the abbey— it is an attack on our decency.

Sister Gertrud comes running, her face aglow. I am in the garden, prepping some of the badly trampled beds for spring planting.

"What happened?" I ask as she draws near.

Sister Gertrud is so young, she reminds me of myself twenty years ago. Unlike me, she has blonde hair, but she is full of energy and devotion for her new life.

At first, it seems the young novice does not wish to speak. She holds on to one of the trellises that support our grapes in summer and peers over the edge of the wall. From up here we have a sweeping view of the Eisack Valley, the vineyards and rock faces. The villages below appear small, like miniatures. When I first arrived, I often imagined I was flying above the world like an eagle.

I just watch Gertrud, whose burning cheeks slowly pale. Patience is one of the things I have learned to cherish, especially since it eludes me at times even now. Benedict's words echo through my head: *Through patience we share in the passion of Christ so that we may deserve also to share in his Kingdom.*

"The men are disgusting," Sister Gertrud finally says. She almost whispers, but my hearing has always been acute, even when my head is wrapped in wimple and veil. For much of the year, it is a welcome protection from the wind.

I say nothing and wait, the shovel in my hand hovering.

Gertrud turns to me and lowers her gaze, her normally brilliant eyes troubled. "I saw their… their… appendage. They just relieve themselves in front of me… even watch me. I tried to turn away, walk quickly, but they called after me and laughed."

I pat Gertrud's arm. "I am so sorry. It is wrong of them. You'd better stay close to us."

"I had to see the Abbess."

Abbess Mayrin still occupies her offices in the main house. I do not know how she stands it, but I think she is trying to keep an eye on the situation, no matter how difficult. Father Schweiggl walks around like his own ghost. He may as well not be here at all.

"It will pass, it must." I remember my own shock the first time I laid eyes on a man's member. To this day, I think of it as a poisonous snake, the way it bites—

"…wrong?"

Sister Gertrud's eyes are on me. Somehow, I have dropped the shovel.

I return to the present. "What?"

"Something is wrong, isn't it?"

"Of course not, go with God, my child. We must discuss these matters with the Abbess after the meal."

Sister Gertrud bows respectfully and hurries back to the guesthouse.

My eyes move upward and yet inward. All those months since Georg recognized me, I have been watching over my shoulder, sneaking around in hopes to avoid him. Mostly, I try to take another sister with me wherever I go—a system the Abbess has suggested and that I welcome more than she realizes.

A long time ago, I came here to find God and a place to feel safe that gave me comfort and a loving community. Now the abbey has turned into a threat. From the inside, not to mention the approaching French army.

Have I been naïve to think God provides answers? Why is he testing us this way?

Because you are strong and he tests those who can bear it.

After *Vespers* and our meal, Abbess Mayrin addresses us all. Even before she opens her mouth, I know she is upset and that what she is going to say will mean more hardship.

"Dearest Sisters, Herr Haspinger has told me today that he expects us to leave in February. He said Bonaparte's army is moving closer and that it is unsafe for us to remain any longer."

"We cannot," breaks from Dorothea's lips. Her white veil, which marks her as a novice, quivers like her voice. "This is our home."

"It is much safer if we leave," Schweiggl's deep voice cuts in.

Easy for you to say. Schweiggl arrived here seven years ago from St. Georgenberg, another monastery.

The Abbess raises a hand. It is not becoming to interrupt, though I want to scream along with Dorothea.

"I have been praying for wisdom," the Abbess says. "If indeed the French army attacks up here, we may find ourselves in the middle of a battlefield. So, I want to leave this decision to each and every one of you. There is no judgment, no matter how you decide."

She pauses. Some place outside, deep voices chuckle, a foreign sound even after seven months of occupation. "Your choices are as follows: You may leave and stay with surrounding farmers. Many of the larger ones will be able to host a sister. You would be alone, but likely safer than here. I have communicated with Bishop von Lodron in Brixen." She looks around the room, which is as quiet as during mass. "He has generously offered Castle Velthurns, his summer residence, to us. Of course, you could go home to your families…"

My mind races as the words of Abbess Mayrin fade. I have only seen Georg from a distance. Still I feel the urge to run far from this man. But how can I leave here? Go home? What is the Abbess talking about? I cannot ever… will not return to my birthplace. Besides, running off feels like abandoning everything I believe in. After all, Sabiona has protected me all this time. Maybe it is my turn to protect her.

"…you do?" Sister Adelheid's face is near. It is not nearly as round as six months ago, her complexion pale.

"What?"

"I asked if you decided… where to go." Adelheid watches me curiously. She reminds me of a girl in school a hundred years ago, one who told lies about me. I only found out from my best friend because she had overheard the girl whisper about me meeting boys in the barn after school so I could kiss them.

Naturally, many of the boys tried to take advantage. I was only twelve and did not know more than the few pecks on the cheek my mother had given me over the years.

"I must retire and pray on it," I say to delay my decision.

"I heard about Bishop von Lodron's charity." Sister Adelheid does not notice my trepidation. "I think I shall make the journey. Sister Dorothea says it is less than a two-hour walk."

I bow and rise wordlessly to take refuge in my room. It is true, I could be living in safety at Velthurns, pray undisturbed by ruffian fighters. But what will happen to the abbey if we all go? Benedict said we should only leave for brief sabbaticals, that we bind ourselves to the community here at Sabiona Monastery. We cannot stay at the bishop's residence for long—we are always guests. Likely, he will travel there himself for the summer.

After night prayer, I seek out Abbess Mayrin in her room. "I cannot leave," I say even as my mind screams at me to see reason. "We must protect the abbey."

The Abbess remains silent, though her eyes ask, "How?"

"Once we go, there is no telling what they will do." My thoughts travel to this morning, when I found several men lingering inside the Church of the Holy Cross, our oldest refugium. Though it is a difficult journey across the open areas and past the soldiers' quarters, I had felt the need to visit. The men were chatting, even resting their muddy boots on top of the pews.

I fear for our sacred vessels, the golden chalice for the blood of Jesus, our candleholders and monstrances, the sculptures and the holy altar clothes.

Abbess Mayrin and I look at each other, I see the helplessness in her face, the same helplessness I feel.

"Maybe the younger sisters should go," I say. "They are more likely to…" In my mind, I see Gertrud in the kitchen, the dirty men around her. It is only a matter of time before… something happens.

Abbess Mayrin slowly sinks onto the only chair. "I will pray on it and we shall decide in the morning."

That night, my cell is quiet, no sounds intrude, and yet I cannot sleep. I will be up again before three for the morning office of *Lauds* prayers. I sense the uncertainty of my sisters through the walls, hear our collectively held breaths. Do our prayers reach God tonight? Will he answer and provide?

CHAPTER FIVE

We are still here. It is March and the men are restless, they often squabble, even fight on occasion. Haspinger's expression is grave as he hastens back and forth. They are constantly doing military exercises, practice target shooting and man-to-man combat while we stay cramped in our guesthouse. Sister Gertrud and Sister Dorothea are helping me in the garden where we keep a few winter crops of onions and kale. I have been sorting my seed collections, trying to imagine my garden to distract myself.

We are nowhere closer to deciding about our living situation. Every day, I pray for clarity, for some kind of sign to help my decision. The snow is melting and any day now, Haspinger will order us to leave.

Sister Gertrud's cheeks are red from the cold wind as she works over the soil. Dorothea is helping me harvest onions for dinner. They are not quite large enough yet, but I do not dare leave them or the men will steal them. They walk around our home like they own it—

"Where is the Abbess?" Haspinger shouts, walking up to us. "She is not in her office."

I drop my basket and hurry to meet him. "Let me find her for you."

"No time, something has happened." Haspinger's

usually self-confident voice trembles a bit, which frightens me more than the prospect of witnessing a battle.

We find the Abbess in our dining room that now also functions as living and meeting space.

Haspinger sinks onto a chair and extends his legs. "We received word that the French army is close. They will arrive here any time, and it is not looking good." Haspinger swallows. "I recommended that you leave. It may be too late now." Anger swings in his voice. "I cannot be responsible for a bunch of nuns. Not now, when we may lose the country to Bonaparte. Your priest… Schweiggl said you would go."

Anger boils up in me. How can Father Schweiggl promise the men what we decide? It is not his decision to make, Sabiona is not his abbey, he is merely a guest. Why do men always think they should order women around? Tell us what to do and how to think?

"What should we do?" The Abbess's words bring me back. She is massaging the wooden cross hanging from her neck, a sure sign she is at a loss. I have got one as well, but only wear it on Sundays when I take a break from the garden or kitchen.

Haspinger straightens again. "Not sure, I must prepare my men."

Outside, voices shout, then at least ten men rush in. "Commander, come quick," one says. "They are already in Klausen."

Haspinger hurries off without another word. Through the window, I see them running toward the main house and the gate. Dread begins to fill me. Those men out there are farmers, they are not thoroughly trained, and few have real weapons, most carry an assortment of scythes, flails, pikes and clubs.

I imagine Bonaparte's army swarming through the village at the foot of the abbey, shooting anyone getting into their way. It is maybe a twenty- to thirty-minute, albeit steep, climb to reach us. Even if there are walls around Sabiona, they can be scaled, the gate overrun. My insides buck, nausea rises from my middle. In that moment, I feel terror, an immediate sense of doom.

Worse is the helplessness. We are trapped in here. Even if we tried to leave this minute, we would encounter the French on our way. Would they kill women… nuns?

The Abbess straightens. "Get the sisters together and have them pack their things. We shall wait here together. Then go to my office and collect my seal, paper and ink."

A bell rings, calling us for *None*, our three o'clock afternoon prayer. Sending a silent plea to God, I catch three sisters on their way to church and give instructions.

When I cross the courtyard on the way to the Abbess's office, I see nobody. But there, along the walls, above the path to the abbey's gate, armed men hide—at least those who have actual guns. More amass in front of the gate and tunnel that leads outside.

In the valley, church bells ring as if a storm has caught them. My ears are tuned to such chimes because they announce prayer. Hearing such wild ringing turns my knees weak. Inside the office, it is quiet. The walls here are thick and embrace me. But it is a false quiet, almost as if I am deaf and unable to watch for danger.

Clutching the leather pouch with the Abbess's things to my chest, I head back outside. And freeze.

Screams and shouts ring out along the wall and beyond. I want to take a closer look, want to see what is unfolding on the other side, but my feet are frozen in place. The men on top are frantically shooting and loading. A man cries out, falls backwards and lies still. I recognize him, his reddened pig's eyes are still, a red stain blooms on his chest.

The noise intensifies. Shots explode into thunder. Several voices bark orders, a man shrieks, another moans, bullets hit rock, ricochet… screams rise from beyond the wall. There is a battle raging at our front door. How long will the men keep the French soldiers at bay? How many are there? My mind is numb and at the same time, my thoughts race, except they have no goal, they just swirl around and get stuck in dark corners.

"Sister Magdalena? Please come with me." Gertrud gently takes my arm and leads me to the guesthouse. Everybody is there, the Abbess rushes up to me.

"Praise God, you are safe. I was afraid…" Abbess Mayrin sinks on a chair. My sisters clutch small packs, a set of clothes, a pair of summer sandals, a towel and bible. Some are crying, some praying. Most stand or sit numbly, waiting for some sign—from us or God.

"I doubt we can leave now," I say. "The path to the abbey is clogged with fighting men."

"But we cannot stay," Sister Augusta says. She has somewhat recovered from her chest ailment, but her coughs remind me of the bark of a large dog—deep and guttural.

The Abbess and I are exchanging glances. We may all die and I am to blame. I should have pressured Abbess Mayrin to leave. It is my fault.

Abbess Mayrin raises both arms. "We remain here until the fighting ceases. And while we wait, we may as well get busy and secure our food reserves—in case we must stay a while."

"How long?" Sister Dorothea cries. "What if they come inside?"

Not if but when. I have no doubt that the French will win. They are just too numerous. I overheard Haspinger saying that the Austrian emperor has not sent troops, apparently he told the Tiroleans to fend for themselves.

"I will go back outside to watch," I say. "It is best to know what happens."

Some sisters urge me to stay, but the Abbess nods. She is aware of my willfulness and though it is sinful, right now is not the time to hide.

After a quick drink of water, I sneak back outside. Immediately, the air is filled with the sounds of fighting and suffering men. I want to clog my ears, but of course that is neither practical with a coif, nor is it safe. I must know what is happening, no matter how difficult. The courtyard and halls near the main house are deserted. As I carefully make my way toward the tunnels and the gate, I am overtaken by Father Schweiggl.

"This cannot continue, I will speak with them," he shouts.

I follow wordlessly and watch as he begins to wave and shout in French. To my surprise, the shooting ceases and from some place across the way, a French voice answers. Soon Schweiggl and the French man exchange calls, until Schweiggl steps outside, hands raised.

A man in uniform meets him halfway. I cannot make out their conversation, but after a while, Schweiggl returns. "They will move inside but promised not to steal or destroy Sabiona. They will not harm you."

"What happened?" Haspinger steps in Schweiggl's way as soon as we are back inside.

"The fight is over," Schweiggl says. "You are to lay down your weapons and leave. I promised them one hundred guilders. We will have no bloodshed."

Haspinger lets out a puff of air. "How will we pay for that?"

"I shall speak to Abbess Mayrin," Schweiggl says. "It is better than having more maimed or dead men. They promised to sign a contract."

"I sure would have wished for you to share your plan *before* you spoke to them." Haspinger squints at Schweiggl. "You do not really believe that the French can be trusted."

The priest's expression grows indignant. "The abbey is our biggest concern. We must protect Sabiona. I will draw up a contract in French."

I can tell Haspinger is fuming, but to his credit, he only nods and rushes off, undoubtedly to collect his men.

Around the corner, soldiers lie on the ground—some wail, some lie still. Blood seeps from their bodies, runs in rivulets, disappears in the gloom of the tunnel. My mind wants to go blank with so much suffering. But I need to be practical, not even praying is an option. These men need help. I rush off to alert my sisters, together we sort through our stores of discarded clothing, towels and sheets that we collect for the poor.

Gertrud, Dorothea and I grab armfuls and return to the bleeding men.

One has a wound on his forehead that bleeds so profusely, his eye sockets are filled with sticky red, his hair and beard saturated. I tear apart a sheet and bind a piece around his head, wipe his eyes clean. The next one's waistcoat is stained dark. I carefully lift the fabric. There's a pool of blood there. The man remains still and when I look up again, his open eyes stare into the sky. I close his lids, mumble a prayer and move on.

This one is young, no more than sixteen, with only a few scraggly beard hairs. He is moaning softly. His right leg above the knee is bleeding, creating a puddle beneath. Again, I tear strips of fabric and carefully pull them through beneath the injured leg. He is bleeding way too heavily to make it much longer. When I tie the cloth, the boy screams. Still, I pull tighter until the bleeding decreases to a trickle. When I look up, he has passed out, his breath ragged.

As I bend over the next man to look for wounds, he takes my hand.

"Sister, I thank you for your kindness. It is too late for me."

I want to say nonsense, but then I see that his vest is torn apart and pieces of entrails show. Bile rises from my stomach, I heave. *You can do this*, my mind comments. I let out a sigh and force a smile.

"Please pray for me, Sister," the man whispers. A sheen lies on his eyes, the sheen of approaching death. I have seen it before… when an older sister passed. I nod and grip the man's hand.

"What is your name?"

"Leopold Weiner."

"I ask you to welcome Leopold into your midst, dear Lord…"

Halfway through my prayer, his hand relaxes. He is

gone.

In that moment, I hear steps rushing up the tunnel toward me. In the shadow of the tunnel, I make out men running. Only when they reach the light do I see the fright on their faces, eyes and mouths gape wide open. Some have no more weapons.

I am still kneeling when the first reaches me, jumps across the bleeding men, and disappears around the corner toward the main house. The others follow as I am staring toward the dark end of the tunnel. It is narrow and long, no more than six feet across, and was meant to keep unwanted visitors out.

Something moves in the shadows, steps echo, march confidently forward… toward me… I do not even have to see them to know that the French army is here.

Throwing a last glance at the bleeding men, I shout at Gertrud and Dorothea. Together we rush between the buildings, down to the guesthouse.

The door is locked, so I knock frantically. "They are here, let us in." Behind me, more cries and shots ring out. *They are coming.*

Ever so slowly, the door opens and the frightened face of the Abbess appears. "Quick, come inside. What happened?"

I sink onto a bench and try to catch my breath. My throat is dry, my chest heaves as if the air is too thin in here.

"You are injured," Sister Adelheid cries, followed by shrieks from around the room.

Only now do I see the state of my hands. They are stained with dried blood. I cringe, but then I realize that my habit is damp as well. More blood. My stomach turns a second time. I swallow several times, take deep breaths. I must hold it together, if not for me then for my sisters.

"We need to wash." I hold out my arms as if they are coated with poison, hardly recognize my voice. But then I remember what Schweiggl did and tell the sisters.

"One hundred guilders?" Abbess Mayrin cries. "How will we afford it?"

In my mind, I go over our budget. I have seen the numbers and we barely get by as it is.

Abbess Mayrin rubs her forehead. "How can he promise them payment we do not have?"

Someone knocks, then yanks the door handle. We freeze.

"Let me in!" Schweiggl's deep voice sounds irritated. Sister Gertrud opens it and the priest marches in. "They will spare us," he announces. "I made peace with them."

As Abbess Mayrin takes Schweiggl aside, Gertrud rushes over to me. Her hands are also red. "Let us go to our rooms. I will wash your tunic."

"I will do it," I say as we enter the cell, though I just want to creep beneath the blanket on my bed. "Just get me my spare from the bag."

As Gertrud disappears, I stare at the whitewashed walls. Only, in my mind, they are red with the blood of the farmers who lost their lives defending Tirol… us. Most of them are likely dead. I wonder what happened to Haspinger. Did the French get him too?

Outside, men shout. I do not speak French, but I know it anyway. Any moment they will break down the door.

"No time to change," I say to Gertrud, who is shaking out my spare habit. "Just put it back for now." I raise my hands and try a smile. "My fingers are clean."

I set my jaw as we return to the kitchen. The doorknob to our guesthouse is under attack, followed by aggressive knocking.

"Alo?" someone shouts. "Open or we shoot."

The Abbess rises from her seat, glances at us, and nods. "I will speak to them."

Wordlessly, I follow Abbess Mayrin to the door.

She turns the key and cracks the door, which is immediately shoved open all the way. Six men in bluish-gray uniforms, with muskets and sabers at the ready, push past us.

"Who is in charge?" one of them says in bad German. He is at least six feet tall and very thin, his eyes as dark as his hair. With the red hat, he is even taller.

"I am," the Abbess says. "We are Benedictine—"

"Do not speak," the man shouts, then signals his men to search the building. We just stand or sit, a few dozen nuns in black and white, and Schweiggl, who all of a sudden appears meek. We have missed prayers again, so I send a quick appeal to God. Surely he sees the peril we are in. We are far from anything that Benedict tells us about welcoming our guests.

"You are nuns," the man says when his soldiers return empty-handed. Did they think we were hiding Tiroleans in our cells? I chew on my lower lip. *Isn't it obvious?*

"This is a convent." Abbess Mayrin stretches herself just a bit, not an easy task because she cannot be more than five feet tall.

"It is ours now." The French man nods at Schweiggl, who has not moved. "Your priest prepares contract." His expression is unreadable, or do I detect a glimmer of satisfaction? I am unprepared for the hatred that prickles in my heart. I am a Benedictine nun, not a common person, held to a higher standard, and yet I want to kick the French man, shout ugly words at him.

He takes a sweeping glance around the room, takes in our meager pile of onions and bread, our traveling bags. "We will need this place for our soldiers. You can go."

For a moment, none of us moves. He has dismissed us like you would scorn a mangy dog.

"It is *our* home," I say. I have never spoken with such venom.

The tall man says something in French that elicits a laugh from his soldiers. They are watching us, many eyes on Sister Gertrud's flawless face. The tall man spits—on our scrubbed floor.

His gaze lands on me. "You lucky we do not kill you."

A shudder runs through me. He looks like he enjoys murdering people… even nuns. I want to tell him about God's wrath, a final reckoning, but Abbess Mayrin places a hand on my forearm.

"We will pack now," she says. "Will you give us an hour to prepare for our journey?"

The tall man's brows draw together like an approaching storm. He laboriously pulls out a watch. "Ten minutes."

He shouts something to his men and they disappear except for a guard who remains in the entry.

Silence settles in the kitchen.

"Abbess Mayrin, we cannot leave," I say. "Contract or not, they will destroy it all."

The Abbess looks at me as if I have suggested wearing French uniforms.

"They will kill us if we do not," Sister Augusta says. Tears run down her gaunt cheeks as she frantically kneads her hands.

"Did you see them look at Sister Gertrud?" Sister Adelheid's eyes are spitting fire.

"Where will we go?" several nuns ask at once.

Abbess Mayrin rubs her forehead. Indecision mirrors on her face.

"We will lose everything," I try again, avoiding the corner where Schweiggl sits silently. My mind returns to the injured and dying near the gate. "What if we offer our help? Take care of the men?"

Voices rise among us. "Phew, they stink… I cannot touch… it is unthinkable… I would rather die… filthy—"

"Enough." Abbess Mayrin's voice cuts through the noise.

"I will stay." The words tumble from my mouth.

"You cannot possibly remain here alone," Abbess Mayrin says.

"We must hurry," Gertrud cries. "The ten minutes will be up any moment."

Rubbing her wooden cross, Abbess Mayrin begins to pace. There is hardly enough room to turn, so she goes three steps one way, then back. I have never seen her this way. Surely none of us have. Benedict says the Abbess will protect and guide her nuns. Right now, I doubt she knows how to.

"I can always leave if things get really bad," I say.

"I will remain with you." Gertrud steps to my side, takes hold of my right hand.

"I will as well." Dorothea, our other young novice, takes my left.

Abbess Mayrin stops in her tracks, then faces the group. "I want you to decide right now, who will go to the bishop's summer residence? It is not far." Most of the nuns raise their hands.

"I could not possibly walk that far." Augusta's voice is defeated. Two other nuns who are in their eighties nod.

"Then you will seek refuge with the farmers in Klausen." Abbess Mayrin looks at me. "Two sisters will accompany Augusta and her elders and then travel to the bishop's residence. I will stay with Sister Magdalena and the novices. We will send word if things change. Now go."

"But it is too dangerous." Augusta's eyes are filled with tears. She is close to the Abbess, they have known each other for more than fifty years.

The door flies open and two regular soldiers march in, waving their muskets. In the close quarters, it looks as if they are ready to skewer us. "Time to leave."

Abbess Mayrin shoos the nuns out of the room. Only Gertrud, Dorothea and I remain.

"What about you?" One of the soldiers eyes us suspiciously. "You go now."

"We want to speak to your lieutenant." Abbess Mayrin's hands are folded tightly. "We are staying."

"He busy."

Abbess Mayrin plops down on the bench in front of the fireplace. "Then we wait."

The French soldier says something to his companion, throws us a nasty glance, and disappears, leaving the one man standing there alone.

The four of us huddle together. "We can help with the men," I say, "but we can also garden and cook. Benedict says *ora et labora.* We will offer our labor so that we can stay in what should be rightfully our home." My mind scoffs. What is rightful when there is a war on—a war fought by men greedy for power and riches? They spend their lives in politics, pass rules and laws how we are supposed to behave. Until war makes all those rules and laws obsolete. In the end, the common people suffer. Every time.

"What about our prayers?" Gertrud's blue eyes are shadowed with storm clouds.

"First things first," I say quietly. "We may have to pray on our own while we work."

CHAPTER SIX

We are still in the guesthouse and share two cells. Abbess Mayrin and I are used to each other, but it is different to live in the small space. The walls no longer listen to me and that stillness I have so come to appreciate eludes me.

When we insisted on staying, that lieutenant with the black hair looked as if he was going to shoot us on the spot. But in the end, he may have had some qualms about murdering innocent nuns, especially since Father Schweiggl has remained as well. So, we have begun to work for the men. Haspinger and all who could walk disappeared. I wonder what happened with Georg. He is not a young man, but he somehow always gets away. We buried some of our Tirolean farmers, and care for some of the others.

Part of the main house has been made into sick rooms as our small infirmary could not hold them all. Many of the men's wounds fester and we watch them grow weaker with fever. Delirious and restless, they mistake us for their mothers, sisters or wives. We pray with them, cool their burning foreheads—there is no doctor here.

We still observe *Compline*, our night prayer, and *Lauds* at three o'clock in the morning. During the day, it has become increasingly difficult to follow our calling. The French do not understand nor care about our way of life. The hallways are littered with rubbish and empty bottles.

Even if I clean the kitchen, it is disastrous again within hours. When I cannot take this twisted new life any longer, I escape into the garden, tend the tiny flowerbed where new leaves sprout on the rosebush. Everywhere are the signs of spring, crocuses and magnolias bloom. Out here I pretend to be at peace, pretend that everything is unchanged.

We never leave Sister Gertrud's side, afraid she may fall prey to the lusty men, now drunken on their victory and the last stores of wine. Nobody knows how long they will stay, communication with them is as difficult as speaking to a goat.

Secretly, we wonder why we have to share two rooms when half the abbey stands empty. It is a relief to *only* have fifty or so French men on our grounds. The other soldiers have left to undoubtedly conquer the remainder of Austria, if not Europe. Bonaparte is hungry to take over the world. Father Schweiggl said he has overpowered the Netherlands and fights in Italy. Prussia and Spain have rushed to sign a peace treaty.

I am feeding Franz, a young Austrian who has lost an eye, a bit of watery soup, when shots ring out. I pat the young man on his sleeve and rush to the window, Sister Gertrud by my side.

Along the high wall, men appear between the battlements. They move stealthy and quick, take cover immediately. I recognize their dress as that of the Tirolean army, think I recognize Haspinger.

They are back.

Laughter rings out—it is my own. Just a few weeks ago, I resented their presence, but now gladness fills me. They have come to kick out the French. It is not over yet.

In the halls, French soldiers scramble. They have become complacent up here. It is easy to let yourself be enveloped by serenity, the majestic mountains topped by an unending sky so blue, it is as if God had used a giant paintbrush of azure.

"What are they doing?" Gertrud whispers. She has been taking care of a French man who was shot in the arm and now burns with fever.

I shrug and grip Gertrud's sleeve. "Making the French leave. Let's remain in here until this is over."

"What is going on?" Franz asks when I resume feeding him. His remaining eye, as green as a conifer forest, anxiously watches me.

"Your friends have returned to kick out the enemy."

A slow smile spreads on Franz's features. His cheek below the missing eye is bruised and swollen, and he soon grows serious again. "Will you tell me what happens, Sister?"

I straighten the boy's blanket. "Of course. Now you'd better rest."

Ever so quietly, I tiptoe to the door and then outside. Few shots are being fired, but there are more and more screams and they come from the other side of the buildings, the side where the monastery perches on a sheer cliff. From up here, it is a free fall for hundreds of feet.

I pass French soldiers lying dead in the courtyard, in front of the Church of the Holy Cross. Their throats have been cut. I rush inside in search of a moment of peace. I must speak to God, ask Him for clarity.

Oh Lord in heaven, I beg your forgiveness for my sins. I do not mean to feel such glee, seeing the French lie dead. We are supposed to love our fellow beings, and yet I cannot find the love in my heart, when they take what is meant for the church, for you, Lord. I beg for your wisdom, your strength and understanding.

I had considered myself beyond such earthly feelings, such deep ugly emotion. My relationships are with God and my sisterly Benedictine community. Now I find that my life crumbles and with it my generous loving heart. I feel fury, even hatred for the intruders who destroy what I love. It is sinful, is it not?

I lower my head further, keep my eyes squeezed shut. *Please God, let me know what is right, what I should do.*

I sign a cross over my forehead and chest, and rise. The altar has been bare since I hid our sacred vessels and cloths.

The door is ripped open and a French soldier rushes

in. It is the skinny tall lieutenant with the black hair. Unlike before, he looks scared, even crazed. He ignores me and hurries to the altar, disappears behind it.

I have not moved more than a few feet toward the exit when the door opens again. Three Tiroleans rush inside. They quickly bend their heads in acknowledgment of this holy place, but then grip their weapons tighter. One carries a musket, the other two pikes.

They look at me questioningly and all I do is turn my head toward the altar.

Moments later, the French man is escorted outside. Instead of heading to the courtyard, the men turn right, to the half wall behind which opens a precipice to the Eisack valley below.

A single scream splits the air as the French soldier disappears over the edge. The Tiroleans hurry off, silence settles. I stand there, frozen in place as a familiar figure marches up to me.

"Thought I would find you here," Georg says. "When I heard there were still nuns left, I knew one of them would be you." His mouth curls upward, but his eyes, still dark and piercing, remain furtive. He has reached me, stands close like lovers would.

I take a step back, then another, but like last time, his hands clamps around my forearm. Squeezes.

The pain is sudden and vicious, but I say nothing. Cannot. The relief I had felt getting rid of the French, being *rescued* by our men, fades. Not even the French treated me like that.

"Leave me be."

Georg leans in, his breath reeks of wine. "We may not have seen each other in a while, but you are mine. Always were."

I suck air, because the grip tightens further, my arm throbs. "I belong to God," I mumble.

"What was that?"

Against my better judgment, I raise my head, lock eyes

with him. So close, I recognize the drink in his features, the sallow skin beneath his eyes, the sharp lines between nose and mouth. "I belong to God," I say. "Let go of my arm."

He huffs, releases another cloud of alcohol fumes. Now he really grins. It is an ugly grin that distorts his features.

"Teiner, I need you at the gate." I recognize Haspinger's voice and turn abruptly. Georg must have been surprised because he lets go of my arm.

"Sister Magdalena?" Haspinger tips his hat. "I thought you and the other sisters left."

I force a smile. "Four of us remained here. We are taking care of the sick."

"That French riffraff?" sneers Georg.

I just look at Haspinger. "Some of your men also. Young Franz… They needed help, it was the only way to remain and keep an eye on Sabiona."

Haspinger nods. "I am sure it was difficult. We are back now, only fifty or so. Georg here volunteered to protect the abbey."

If you only knew. "Abbess Mayrin is here as well," I say aloud. "We could not let it go." I look over the ransacked grounds, the newly hung Tirolean flag, the bloodstains on the walkways. "How much longer will it take?"

Haspinger's brows draw together and something cold creeps up my back. "I am afraid it is not over. Napoleon's army is vast." He glances at Georg, a glint of curiosity in his eyes because Georg has remained by my side. "Teiner, they are waiting."

Georg nods obediently and hurries off. I cannot help but stare after him. Hidden by the sleeves of my habit, I rub the soreness in my forearm. Is that hate I feel?

Haspinger has not noticed and bends closer. "I heard that more soldiers under General Joubert are on the way. They won a decisive battle at Tarvis, captured three thousand, five hundred Austrians." He sighs. "I was hoping to return to my studies, but it does not look good."

I stare at the young man with the curved nose, realize

that he is dreaming of a different life as well.

"What do you want to do?"

For the first time, he smiles. "I want to become a priest."

I realize that I am staring open-mouthed now when he breaks into laughter. "Yes, Sister, I aspire to follow God's word—just like you."

"Then I will pray for a quick return to your studies."

He wordlessly tips his hat and rushes off. Deep in thought, I walk back to our guesthouse. With just the four nuns and no more French in the house, our building has taken on a hush. How do you reconcile being a soldier and killing men with priesthood? Can you do God's work on a battlefield? Would He ever demand such a task from a priest… or a nun? Doesn't it say in Matthew, *Love your enemies and pray for those who persecute you…?*

Who am I to judge? I, who just moments ago, felt such relief, witnessing Bonaparte's soldiers being tossed to their deaths. And there is Georg, an apparition from my past, a man I wish to disappear.

I never imagined being tested like this, being split in half by my beliefs. I collect more onions from the garden, my ears on alert, in case Georg is looking for me. Our evening meal will be onion soup and bread. It is all I have left because our weekly deliveries have ceased under the French occupation.

"I will go to Klausen," I say to the Abbess after dinner. I have considered telling her about Georg, but what can she do? Besides, she has enough on her mind to keep us going. "We are near the end with our provisions. The Tirolean men will need sustenance."

Abbess Mayrin takes my hand. "It is dangerous, Magdalena. What if there are more French lurking about?"

"I will go with you." Gertrud's usually lustrous eyes seem permanently darkened.

"I shall go alone," I say.

"The village is in disarray," says Abbess Mayrin. "I spoke with one of the fighters whose father has a farm. After the French, I wonder if they have supplies left. Maybe we should wait a few days."

For what, I want to say. Instead, I bend my head. "Yes, Mother."

CHAPTER SEVEN

It is peaceful. I haven't seen Georg in days and the few dozen other soldiers no longer bother me. I am back in the garden, planting a few more spring crops: kohlrabi, cauliflower and salad. Tomorrow I must prune three apple and pear trees. I used to have help from two lay sisters, but none of the other sisters have returned yet. It is a beautiful day, the sun's rays intense on my cheeks. Here within the walls, the wind is calm. Once in a while, I lift my face into the sun. At last, things are looking up.

The bell rings for *Vespers*, so I rush inside to wash and pray. Today, we meet in the kitchen, where Sister Dorothea has cooked another soup. I have been teaching her for a while, but she is not picking up recipes as quickly as I would like. Once again, I detect too little salt and a lack of herbs. We still have a decent store of dried thyme, oregano, basil and parsley, which do wonders to a meal when there is little variety. The bread from this morning's bake has not been stored properly, so it is dry and crumbly. I shall have a word with Dorothea later.

We have been skipping *Sext*, our midday meal, and I am hungrier than usual. The four of us sit across from each other, the scraping of our bowls the only sounds. Speaking during meals is not allowed, though today I have the urge to discuss our situation.

I swallow the last bread, drink water to chase away the dryness in my throat. It used to be customary to have dessert on weekends, but we have no more suitable fruit. The last canned plums, pears and apples disappeared into French stomachs. Walnuts and raisins are also gone.

I rescued a few bottles of wine for Sunday service, now hidden behind the logs by the kitchen stove.

"Will we move back to the main house, should we send word to our sisters?" Gertrud asks, as she clears the plates. "Maybe they could return. We cannot possibly care for the abbey with four people. Surely the Tiroleans will depart soon to tend to their fields."

"We do not even know where they all went," I say. "Also, I want to go to the village tomorrow. I am worried we will run out of supplies soon."

Abbess Mayrin sighs. "It is true. In the rush, we only know some of our sisters went to the bishop's summerhouse. I shall send word with the men when they leave." She produces a small smile I know is forced. The Abbess does not expect the men to leave. "I shall ask Herr Haspinger about a departure date."

I lean forward. "And can I go tomorrow?"

Abbess Mayrin smiles weakly. "Tomorrow, then."

I do not know why I am so excited to depart this time. Other than an occasional walk through the vineyards and an ever-rarer visit to the village, I never go anywhere. I do not feel comfortable being outside the walls. They feel like protective arms that shield me from the world.

Of course, that is an illusion. I know that now… after the Austrians… and the French.

But I am the cellarin. I must take care of our nourishment.

After three o'clock prayer, I return to bed to rest. But this morning, sleep eludes me. I get back up before six to wash and attend the office of *Prime*. Afterwards, we drink peppermint tea while Abbess Mayrin discusses the day.

Gertrud and Dorothea will return to the infirmary, I will leave after *Terce* and our morning meal.

"I will help you with the bread," I say to Dorothea, who is spreading flour all over the table. Her habit is dusted white, so are her hands. She just nods without looking at me. "I wanted to speak with you about our evening meal," I say, trying for a smile. "I was hoping we could use flour to thicken the soup. With just the onions, it is awfully thin. And we could use a bit more salt, we have ample stores."

The wooden baking pan clatters to the floor as Dorothea abruptly faces me. "Everyone can salt their own bowl."

"It is inefficient. What is bothering you, child?" I ask. Dorothea cannot be older than twenty.

"I am not your child."

"I did not mean—"

"I am tired of being told what to do. I am tired of the endless chores, I cannot bear it."

"Have you spoken to the Abbess?"

"Why should I?"

Dorothea sounds like a petulant child.

"Because Abbess Mayrin has much experience with the challenges of our faith."

I do not know if the young novice hears me, but she slaps together our breads, as if she wants to beat them.

I decide to help clean the mess and speak to the Abbess later.

I leave the guesthouse behind Gertrud and Dorothea who are heading to the infirmary. On a whim, I follow them to look in on one-eyed Franz.

His cheeks have a bit of color and he smiles when he recognizes me. "Good to see you, Sister. I already ate breakfast."

"I am so glad you are feeling better." I kneel next to the boy and smooth his blanket. "Maybe you will get to go home soon?"

A smile broadens Franz's face. "I hope so." Then his brows draw together again. "What day is it?"

"April 4."

"Spring planting has already started," he mumbles. "I will leave as soon as Captain Haspinger lets me go. I doubt I am much good aiming a gun."

I pat him on the shoulder and straighten. "I shall see you later tonight?"

Franz sinks back on his pillow, his good eye on me. "Thank you, Sister, I do not think I would have survived without your care."

I shake my head. "God is merciful. I had nothing to do with it."

He fervently shakes his head. "He and you together perhaps?"

I smile and turn to leave when he calls to me. "Sister, I wanted to tell you…" When I face him again, a tear drips down his temples into the pillow. "You remind me of my mother. She was a good woman."

"Is she… dead?"

"Died of consumption two years ago."

I kneel once more and look at the young man. If I had married, I would likely be a mother, only to send my son into war. A shadow seems to fall across the room, a darkening as if clouds have covered the sun. Worry grips me then, a feeling of doom so strong, my breath sticks in my throat. I have to force out the words, "I am very sorry, I shall pray for her as well." A church bell rings. I will miss *Terce*, our nine o'clock prayer. "I'd better go."

Still reeling about the sudden uneasiness, I take a shortcut between the buildings. I must concentrate on my journey to Klausen. What will I do if Georg sees or follows me? I hope Haspinger's orders keep him busy.

Sister Dorothea is sitting on a bench next to a soldier with a bandaged leg. Only when I draw near do I notice the young man caressing Dorothea's hand. But what surprises me more is the expression in his eyes, a mix of devotion and happiness. The man is in love with our sister.

I would not have thought much of it, after all, it is understandable if a young man falls for the woman who takes care of him. But when Dorothea notices my presence, she yanks her hand from his grasp. Her cheeks glow and her eyes still sparkle from the attention of the young soldier. I simply nod and rush past, not sure what I could or should have said.

Of course, it sometimes happens that a young novice leaves us before taking her permanent vows. It is a simple life up here, which in its simplicity can be challenging. Most women who join the convent have reasons all their own. *Like you*, my mind comments.

At the gate, ten or so men keep watch, Georg among them. I ignore his sullen glance and lower my head, rush past and force my attentions back to Dorothea.

It is rare that a novice leaves because of love. Usually, they experience doubt about the seclusion they commit to for life. Even if they are—

"Get back! Quick, inside," a man shouts, tearing me from my thoughts. The wall along the path to the left is at least fifteen feet tall and I at first cannot tell where the voice is coming from.

"Up here, Sister." Fear swings in the man's voice. "The French are coming. It is not safe."

I stare at the bearded face seemingly flying above me. *Not again. Please, dear Lord, I cannot do this again.*

The Lord does not hear me.

A shot explodes nearby, and the man on top disappears. I swivel on my heels, lift my habit enough to run back toward the gate and tunnel. Behind me, more rounds are fired. Men shout, feet scramble. The gate, where is the gate? One of the sentries who waved at me earlier calls to me, but in the racket, I cannot understand him. Ten more yards… why am I so slow? Suddenly, red spreads on the man's high forehead. His eyes are open and a bit surprised as he sinks slowly to the ground. By the time I pass him, he is staring into the sky.

I think I am yelling something at the men who rush forward and pass me in the tunnel. My gut tells me they will be too late. They will not stop the French. Not this time.

I do not know how I am still breathing, but somehow, I am flying up the stairs into the infirmary. Sister Gertrud and Dorothea are both sitting with patients, so I call to them to follow me. This is no place for a nun. When Bonaparte's army arrives, they will likely kill everyone, including the sick. They will not have forgotten the Tiroleans throwing the French men off the mountain.

Franz rests peacefully, his good eye closed. I shudder, thinking he will not live another hour. And yet I can do nothing.

"What is happening?" Gertrud cries.

"I want to stay." Dorothea still kneels next to the young man she held hands with earlier.

"The French are back," I say. "We must hide."

"What about them?" Dorothea cries. Her voice is sharp, full of accusation. What indeed?

Our patients, those who are well enough, stir. Franz wakes and scans the room, before his good eye comes to rest on me. Wordlessly, I wave at Dorothea. "We must go now."

"Please stay," the man next to her pleads.

I recognize the conflict in Dorothea's expression. Outside, shouts ring out, more shots are fired. Not long now.

I hurry to Dorothea and whisper, "The French will not spare us if we stay here." They may not anyway.

Reluctantly, Dorothea accepts my outstretched hand.

In the courtyard, men are running or limping, loading guns and yelling. I breathe a sigh of relief when I recognize Abbess Mayrin hurrying our way.

"Thank the Lord, you have not left," she cries.

More soldiers crowd past us into the tunnel as we stumble toward the guesthouse, Georg among them. I am numb, unsure what I wish for. If he is killed, my life becomes easier, the worry about his glowering presence would cease. Yet how can I wish death upon anyone? I am a nun, married to God, I am supposed to have only goodness in my heart.

But I realize it is an illusion. Humans, no matter what they seek, carry good and evil. Even nuns and priests do. *You are only a nun in name*, my mind comments.

Shots are fired, men cry out in agony: short gasps, high-pitched wails and low guttural moans. The air is thick with the smoke of gun powder. Panic creeps through me, I do not feel my legs, my throat is tight. There is no good place now. We are trapped like the Tiroleans. God is the only one who will protect us now.

Our progress to the guesthouse is slow, Abbess Mayrin's breath rattles. I hold on to her elbow, so she doesn't fall.

The man who warned me earlier is no longer at his post on top of the wall. A rope connected to a hook appears on top. Then another and another. The French are mounting an attack along the outer path.

"Hurry," I cry. Only when we throw shut the door to the guesthouse do I realize that my lungs are about to burst. Together we move the wooden armoire from the kitchen in front of the door. At least we have enough water to last for two days.

"The windows," Gertrud cries. "Close the shutters." Indeed, two windows in our kitchen open into the garden. Anyone can simply break them and move inside.

Abbess Mayrin sinks to her knees. "Let us pray."

CHAPTER EIGHT

Beyond the walls of the guesthouse, the noise swells and ebbs. It is a mixture of blasts and voices, cries of agony next to victorious shouts. I want to stick my fingers in my ears, yet I sit silently next to my sisters. We each have folded our hands in prayer, though this is unlike any prayer I have ever done.

The bones of my knuckles ache from the pressure exerted—I could easily press a lemon between my palms. Not only does God not hear us, I feel utterly helpless. Despite my tunic that hides my body, ears and hair, I feel naked.

I know this feeling, thought I never thought I would experience it again… climbing in the dark, slipping on the ice, just inches away from the precipice of the mountain and certain death.

"What will happen to us?" Gertrud's voice is so small, I hardly recognize it.

Abbess Mayrin pats her hand. "I will speak with them once they appear."

How much time has passed? The noise outside has died down, the silence worse than the shouts.

Dorothea stands up. "Maybe we should show ourselves, look after the sick."

"You must not." Abbess Mayrin grips Dorothea's arm

as if she will never let go. "It is dangerous, let them come here."

"But what if the men need us?"

I want to tell Dorothea that *her* young man is likely dead, but I say nothing. I see the one-eyed boy, Franz, before me, his happy smile, when he thought he would go home to his family soon. The pressure on my heart clogs my throat with unshed tears.

Footsteps grow louder outside. A knock follows, then somebody attempts to open the door. The heavy cupboard shudders, voices shout in French.

Then several things happen at once. Something explodes, the door breaks apart, the cupboard splinters, and dishes crash to the floor.

Four French men in blue coats and white pants rush toward us, muskets at the ready.

In unison, the four of us sink to our knees and lower our heads. "God have mercy," we cry. At least that is what I think I say, because I cannot hear anything but the hammering of my heart and the rushing of blood in my ears.

A pair of black boots appears in my vision. The leather is stained and slick as if the wearer has waded through a sea of blood. "Just you four?" he asks in bad German.

I raise my head and face the man, so does Abbess Mayrin. The French soldier is surprisingly short and stout, his chin darkened with stubble. Harsh lines run from his nose to his mouth, the lips no more than a thin bluish streak.

"Yes," we say at the same time.

The soldier shouts something at his men, who disappear down the hallway. I quake, thinking that I had considered hiding Franz in here.

Moments later, the soldiers reappear empty-handed.

The man who addressed us marches to the door, where he turns to face us. "Stay away. This… is ours now."

Silence settles as we look at each other. Unable to kneel another second, I decide to investigate the door. There is a hole where the lock used to be—impossible now to close properly.

Abbess Mayrin wakes from her rigidity. "Gertrud and

Dorothea, would you please sort out the closet? It is of no use, so we might as well burn the wood."

While the young sisters pick through the broken china and clean the floor, the Abbess takes me aside. "I hate to put this on you, but we must secure our food supply. I doubt the French will share."

"I shall work the garden as before. Maybe we can reason with the commander, offer to share some of the produce against grains and other food." *What about now?* I want to add. We have hardly enough to last us a week. That is why I wanted to visit the farmers in the valley. But I cannot leave now. Even if I did, they would likely stop me from re-entering. And any food the farmers delivered—if they are still alive— would not reach us.

Only one thing is better. Georg has left. He may even be injured or dead.

A sigh rises from Abbess Mayrin's chest. "Listen, sisters, we will need to stay indoors as much as we can… keep away from the men."

"What about our church?" Gertrud cries. The monastery church is our most private sanctuary, though I have always loved the old Church of the Holy Cross best.

"We cannot risk it," the Abbess says. "None of the churches will be safe. They are too far from here. You would have to cross the courtyard, pass by the main house."

"Not even the chapel?" Dorothea says quietly.

The Chapel of Mercy is located inside the Church of Our Lady at the bottom of the abbey's property.

"Too far." Abbess Mayrin straightens. "I will not even return to my offices."

"What about the men?" Dorothea says. She has been standing by the window, not saying a word.

"Which men?" I ask.

Dorothea turns to face us, her eyes wet with tears. "The sick ones. They will need our help."

Abbess Mayrin and I share a look. "Too dangerous," she says. "Besides…"

"Besides what?" Dorothea asks.

The Abbess turns to the fireplace. "Nothing. We'd better prepare a meal. Will you help me?"

I have heard enough and hurry outside.

The sun is covered behind milky clouds, the air has cooled since this morning. A chill lies in the air. Somewhere near the main house, fires smolder. The columns of smoke are thick and acrid. I hurry in the other direction toward my garden. I need help badly, at least five sisters to prepare the beds. I have maybe one, if Gertrud is brave enough to join me. Along the walls overlooking the path and the valley below, French soldiers stand every ten feet and keep guard.

Was it just a few hours ago that I planned to go to the village?

I lower my head and march into the shed where we keep gardening tools. My usual serenity has left me, my joy of being close to nature and God up here. Half blind with tears, I rummage through my seed packets. Some tumble to the ground.

"Damn," escapes from my mouth as I kneel to find them. That is when I hear the sound like a suppressed giggle. What in the world…? I freeze and stare into the gloom, try to keep calm. In the back of the shed we keep burlap sacks for potatoes and onions. Ever so slowly, I straighten and creep toward the dark corner. There is no sound now, but I sense a presence.

Quickly, I grasp a rake and poke the pile of burlap while yelling, "Who is in there?"

"Please, Sister," a quiet voice says. The burlap moves and the face of Franz, the one-eyed boy, appears.

The rake falls from my fingers and I clamp a hand in front of my mouth to keep myself quiet.

"I mean no harm," the boy says. "I just had to laugh hearing you swear. I have never heard a nun—"

"What are you doing here?" I cry. "Are you out of your mind? The French are everywhere."

"I heard them and when I saw your expression, I knew

I had to do something." The boy's good eye glitters with tears. "All I want is to go home."

Outside, voices grow louder. I put a forefinger on my lips and motion the boy to hide once more. Then I step outside, rake and seeds in hand.

Not twenty-five feet from me, three French soldiers approach. They are young and look cocky, the kind of young men my father served beer to in his pub. They are talking animatedly until they see me.

"What you do?" one of them shouts. He has a handsome face, his eyes a bright blue, his nose fine and thin, but all that is immediately forgotten for the cruel mouth, which turns downward at the corners. I can see the aggression in his eyes, hear it in his voice. He is spoiling for another fight. Not to mention what he will do to the boy hiding in the shed. I must not give him away.

I lower my head in greeting and say, "Praise the Lord, I am gardening so we can harvest God's bounty."

One of the other young men makes some remark I do not understand, which seems to spur the aggressive one on. "What you have there?" he asks, pointing the bayonet of his musket at my seed basket.

"Seeds."

"What seeds?" The men have reached me and the aggressive one rips the basket from my hand. The little sacks I have carefully sorted and marked tumble to the ground.

The man rips one open, seeds fly. "Mmmh," he mocks, "God's bounty."

I want to kick the man against his shin, want to smack my fist into his gleeful face. Stupid and mean are a sure recipe for disaster. So, I do nothing, just stand there crying inside about the men's idiocy. The three laugh as if there has been joke, so I bend low, intend to pick up our future food.

Without warning, the boot of the cruel man lands on my fingers. I stare at the black scuffed leather as the heel slowly grinds down. Searing pain shoots through my left hand, up my wrist, into my arm, up to my shoulder. The men laugh, but despite my agony, I remain completely silent.

Behind me, somebody shouts. It is sharp and commanding and the boot immediately lifts away. All three men stand at attention, while I still kneel, my left hand muck-encrusted and fiery. I stare at it as if it does not belong. My fingers already begin to swell. I need to cool them with water, test if they are broken, find Arnica to speed the healing, but I cannot move.

Behind me, a discussion ensues—the name Louis falls several times, I assume it is the attacker—before the three men march off in a hurry.

Only then do I turn and recognize the short and square commander who broke through the door of our guesthouse. We exchange a glance and I recognize the turmoil in his eyes—he wants to help me, yet it is not proper. I detect the tiniest nod, before he marches off behind the other three.

Ever so slowly, I rise. The movement and lowering my injured hand send darts of pain up my arm. I cannot work now, not like this. And there is the young man still hidden in the burlap. He will never make it out of here. Not on his own. Probably not even if we help—which will endanger us… my sisters.

Slowly, I walk back into the shed and close the door. "It is safe for the moment," I whisper.

The boy crawls from his hiding place before his gaze falls on the bruised hand I am cradling with the other. "What happened?"

I shrug. "Cruel French." A sigh escapes me.

Franz huffs. Even in the gloom, I sense his fury. "If I only had a weapon."

Despite the pain, I grin. "What would you do against so many?"

"How many are there?"

"The commander said there are four hundred of them."

The boy's cheeks drain until they look as pale as his bandage. "What will I do?"

I look at him, want to reassure him, but no words leave my mouth. Lying is a sin. "Promise me you'll stay here. I will bring you water and food." Where did that come from? How can I help this boy and endanger my dear sisters?

How can I not?

CHAPTER NINE

In the afternoon, I manage to smuggle a bit of bread and water outside. Benedictine nuns always eat together in silence, so I wait until after *None* at three o'clock before starting my gardening. I have to pretend, because my hand feels like a set of overstuffed sausages about to explode. At least I am thankful for the wide tunic and long sleeves, because they allow me to hide things.

I have not told the Abbess of my ordeal—my left hand feels as if it is possessed, I cannot hold anything with it. She has too much to worry about already. Benedict would not approve, but I do not want to add more burdens.

French soldiers are lounging in the gardens, some rest on the ground, some sit in groups. I pick my way carefully toward the shack, make a detour between the beds that usually hold beans… any second, I expect one of the men to call out, or worse: follow me.

Anxiety rises, an ugly bitter fog inside of me, I am unequipped to fight. Up here, we have never had to struggle with man's cruelty. It was something that happened far away, in some village or other country—another life… the past. Now malice has moved into the abbey. My abbey.

Shutting the door of the hut, I fill my lungs with air and call out with a low voice. "Franz?"

The burlap moves and the one-eyed boy crawls from the shadows. I bend low to hand him the bread, which he chews and swallows quickly, washes it down with the water.

"I will try to get more after dinner," I say. "It is just… I cannot come here too often or the French may become suspicious."

"Of course, thank you, Sister… Magdalena."

I throw him what is hopefully a smile before straightening. "I'd better go now."

He nods and creeps back into the shadows.

To keep my cover, I grab a hand rake and a single bag of salad seeds. But as soon as I kneel, my hand begins to throb. Sharp nails hammer the bone inside until I gasp. I rake a bit with my right, put down the tool, and attempt to open the tiny cloth bag. Impossible.

How could I take my two healthy hands for granted? I will not be any good in the gardens and we will not eat this summer. I realize that we will have to leave. The few of us cannot possibly stay here when we cannot produce anything to eat.

I have to tell the Abbess. Now.

Head low, I hurry back to the shack, quietly deposit my tool and return to the guesthouse.

The Abbess looks up, surprised. She knows I spend every available moment outdoors.

"I must speak to you," I say quietly. When Abbess Mayrin leans back from the book she has been studying, I sink onto the bench across from her. Slowly and carefully, I uncover my mangled hand, which has taken on the color of ripe plums.

Abbess Mayrin claps a hand in front of her mouth. "What happened?"

"A soldier stepped on it." Now that the situation replays in my head, tears press. "I cannot manage the garden."

A puff escapes Abbess Mayrin. She is red in the face now, her mouth opens, then clamps shut. She carefully lifts my wrist and places my injured hand on her palm. "Can you move your fingers?"

I ask my fingers to move. Thumb yes, forefinger yes, middle finger yes, ring finger… Hello? Move. But the finger just quivers.

"It may be broken." Abbess Mayrin's brows scrunch. "We shall have to fix it ourselves." She straightens and asks Gertrud to find supplies. In earlier times, we might have sent word for the doctor who lives in the village.

As the young nun carefully splints and wraps my finger, Abbess Mayrin marches to the door, mumbling, "I will have a word with them…"

At the door, she turns abruptly. "Tomorrow, you will take Gertrud and Dorothea with you. Teach them what to do." She turns in a circle. "Where is Sister Dorothea?"

The three of us look at each other.

"She said she needed a bit of air," Gertrud offers.

"When was that?" I cry.

Gertrud looks at us—guilt in her beautiful eyes. "It… has been a while."

"Child, you—" Abbess Mayrin stops herself. "I must find her immediately."

"I will come with you," I say, even though I would much rather rest my arm.

"What about me?" Gertrud cries.

"You will prepare our dinner," the Abbess says with a firm voice. "Do not leave this house, unless I give permission."

Gertrud lowers her gaze and nods.

Thankfully, the Abbess is rather slow these days, because fatigue and worry make my bones weak. After confirming that Dorothea is not in the garden, we walk toward the main buildings… past assemblies of soldiers who stare at us, whistle or shout things in French I imagine are insults.

At the entry to the main house, a guard steps into our way.

"I need to speak to your commander," Abbess Mayrin says.

The soldier squints at us. "He busy."

"It is urgent."

The guard stares at us with undisguised contempt, but opens the door and speaks to a man right inside. Obviously, they have stationed sentries at every threshold.

My thoughts return to Franz. How can I enter the hut tomorrow when Gertrud and Dorothea are with me? The boy must leave as soon as possible, but how? The entire abbey swarms with French soldiers eager to kill.

"Come," a voice orders.

We hurry after a man who is walking so fast, I have to support the Abbess to keep up.

"In here." The man stops at Abbess Mayrin's former office, now adorned with a French flag.

Behind the desk, the short square man sits. He is unshaven, so his chin and cheeks look black in the low light.

"What is the matter?" The commander looks none too pleased to see us.

"I need your help. We are missing one of our nuns," Abbess Mayrin says. "I am afraid something has happened to her." She hesitates, but then firmly says, "She was *caring* for a sick man before you arrived. She may have tried to see him again."

The commander's eyes are filled with scorn now. "You do realize that we are at war?"

"I want—"

The man raises a hand to cut Abbess Mayrin off. "Your nun was helping an enemy, *our* enemy?"

"Surely you can find it in your heart… he was hurt and she meant no harm… it is our way. Just as we help *your* injured men."

"Abbess Mayrin, is it?" The commander's voice is grave. "I cannot vouch for your sisters if they act carelessly. My men are… soldiers… men, four hundred of them."

My mind spins: four hundred vengeful soldiers against four of us… and one hidden Tirolean boy. "Can we at least look for her?" I ask. "Surely she has to be somewhere."

The commander turns his gaze to me. "She asked for

it."

"Surely you are not suggesting that Sister Dorothea is a threat? Or plans to attack your soldiers?" I fire back. "She is a Benedictine nun married to God and this is her home. Our home."

"Was," the commander barks. "You may not have noticed, but Austria is at war with France. French men died up here, were thrown off the mountain." He points a thumb over his shoulder.

Anger broils beneath my wimple, so hot I want to rip it away. "We have nothing to do with this."

Abbess Mayrin puts a calming hand on my forearm. "The cloister belongs to the church. We did not want *any* men up here and I am responsible for my nun. Sister Dorothea is a novice, a young woman—"

"All right." The commander straightens. "We go."

He marches past us, rips open the door, and shouts something at the two men in the hallway. One of them remains, the other walks behind us.

The corridor stretches, past the kitchen and dining room, the meeting areas—all filled with dozens of blue coats—down the stairs through the courtyard, up the short flight to the sick room.

A French soldier leaning heavily on a cane rests in the doorway. Behind are the beds, now filled with men I do not recognize.

The commander barks something at a soldier dispensing a salve from a brown bottle onto a man's backside, his exposed buttocks a bloody red. I recognize the bottle, made the medicine myself from goldenrod and sheep's fat to heal wounds and burns.

The man eyes us briefly, then shrugs and says something I do not understand.

The commander's expression darkens a bit more before he turns on his heels and motions us to follow.

Again, we walk, down the halls, up a flight of stairs, down another. The floors are filthy with mud and it smells of excrement. The abbey was overtaxed with a hundred seventy Tiroleans. Now there are four hundred men. I cannot imagine the state of our outhouses—nor do I want to. But my nose never lies.

When we turn another corner, I make out voices. Drunken voices who bellow and whistle. Fifty feet farther, a man scrambles away and shouts something. The bellowing and whistling stop. By the time we arrive, it is quiet.

My heart sinks as we enter the shadowy space that once was our library. Books and parchment scrolls lie helter-skelter on the ground. The air is thick with smoke from dozens of pipes and alcohol, the men's faces pale and turned toward us.

On one of the desks that served as study areas lies Sister Dorothea, her habit lifted to expose her thighs, her white socks still stretched to her knees. They match the white veil, the sign of her novice status, now splattered with blood as crimson as the little red cross on her coif. It covers half of the young woman's face. Strands of auburn hair have come loose, the glowing color so gaudy against the black and white. Her eyes are closed, her right one puffy and bluish.

The commander shouts something fiery and several men scramble to cover Dorothea's legs. A low moan rises from the girl's throat, a moan that makes my blood go cold as it takes me back… back into that black hole I had hidden so well from myself. Tears blur my vision as I rush past the men, shove some out of my way, to help Dorothea sit.

"I am here," I whisper. "Let us get you out of here."

When one of the men attempts to touch her, I shoot him a searing glance. He lowers his head as I help Dorothea stand.

Meanwhile, I hear the Abbess speak to the commander. I only hear bits and pieces like… disgusting… God's wrath… abomination… Nuns are not supposed to swear, but right now, I admire Abbess Mayrin for her self-control.

Somebody hands me Dorothea's shoes, which I put on her feet one at a time. It is a struggle because I have only one good hand, the left throbs angrily. Dorothea appears only half conscious, so I wrap one arm around her waist and guide her toward the door.

"Wait." Abbess Mayrin walks to my side and lifts the sleeve of my habit and addresses the commander once more. "This is what your men did to Sister Magdalena. She is our cellarin, she grows the food you undoubtedly want to eat this summer."

I have never heard a sharp word from Abbess Mayrin's mouth, but right now, she is formidable. "My nuns are here to be close to God," she says, enunciating every word. "This is *their* home. You have no right to abuse them, not even in war. I shall pray for your salvation, because, right now, I cannot see how God will forgive such a travesty."

Together we leave the room and lead Sister Dorothea down the path and toward the guesthouse. Four guards follow us twenty feet behind, undoubtedly as protection.

CHAPTER TEN

Sister Dorothea is in bed. I helped her wash and change, but she has not uttered a word. She stares at the wall, holds and kneads the wooden cross between her fingers.

I want to know what happened and, at the same time, I dread the truth.

"How is she?" Abbess Mayrin says from the door.

"Not well," I whisper. With a pang, I remember Franz, who is still hiding in the shed. I must bring him food and drink or he will be too weak to escape.

Ha! He will never get away from here. Not with hordes of enemy soldiers watching every mouse.

Our meal is silent as usual, but today I do not gain any peace from it. It is as if a blackish cloud hovers in our rooms and snuffs out the air we breathe. Gertrud hardly touches her food, her cheeks are tearstained and blotchy.

Still, I have not told the Abbess about Franz. I cannot when she is already so burdened. But how can I allow the young man to be slaughtered?

Gertrud whispered to me about a large grave she discovered this afternoon. She picked a few herbs for our soup and watched a dozen French throw men into a hole and cover it. Undoubtedly, the young Tirolean whom Dorothea liked is among the dead.

I cross myself and look at the ceiling. Please, dear Lord, there is so much bloodshed, so much heartache. When will it end? Now Dorothea is sick in her mind from the things the French did to her. It is my fault. I should not have tolerated them remaining here with me.

After dark, I slip outside, bread and soup hidden under my habit. It is quiet, though lights shine in almost all the windows of the main house. The moon is thin and pale and offers little illumination. Yet I know my way, even if I were blind. Somewhere uphill, a man coughs. *I am not alone. Never alone.*

Now that it is dark and there is no distraction, the stench of urine and excrement returns full force. I will pick lavender as soon as it blooms to at least cleanse the air inside our guesthouse. Gertrud mentioned she saw men toss the contents of their night pots over the edge. Soon, it will be impossible to live here.

The door to the hut squeaks slightly as I close it behind me. I cannot risk lighting a candle, so I call into the dark, "Franz?"

"Yes," comes a thin voice. Is it my imagination or does he sound frail?

"I have food," I whisper.

Something rustles and I feel a presence moving toward me, then a light touch.

"Thank you, sister." I hand Franz the food and lean back. Like last time, he seems to chew and slurp quickly. When he hands back the bowl, I feel him trembling. "I cannot do it much longer, Sister. I am sorry. Tomorrow, I will surrender."

"No, you must not," I cry. "They have… killed all the others from the sick room."

A groan rises between us. Then silence settles, only our breathing rattles loud in the darkness. "I will find a way," I say at last. "Please promise me you'll wait. Just another day?"

The boy says nothing.

"Please," I say again.

"I will wait."

I touch his arm and turn to leave. "I will return in the morning."

"Thank you, Sister."

CHAPTER ELEVEN

All night, I lie awake. It is not only my hand throbbing or Sister Dorothea's suffering, I must find a way for Franz to leave.

"Please, God, hear my prayers. I must save this boy, just this one."

But God is silent and by morning, I am no wiser.

I wash before six o'clock to observe the office of *Prime*. Even if my bones are full of dread and I do not want to move, my mind is trained to be awake. I quickly check on Sister Dorothea, find her staring at the wall like last night. Has she even moved? Her eyes are open and yet unseeing, and she has not touched her food.

"Dorothea," I say quietly. "It is Magdalena, your sister. Will you not eat?"

The girl does not appear to hear me, so I wander into the kitchen. Abbess Mayrin sits, hands folded, in front of the fire.

"I always thought I would spend my entire life up here," she says. When she looks up, there are tears on her cheeks. I sink next to her and take her hand in mine.

"I thought so too. Now God is mute to our suffering."

"Maybe he wants us to leave," Abbess Mayrin says after a while. "It is too dangerous. They almost killed Sister Dorothea, they are laying waste to our abbey. We must move on and find shelter elsewhere, at least for a while."

I look at the older woman who is not just the Abbess, but my friend, a woman I have trusted for a very long time. "I think you should take Dorothea to a safe place, maybe find a doctor to help her." I squeeze her fingers with my good hand. "I will remain here."

I am surprised to hear my own words, yet I know in my heart that I must remain.

Abbess Mayrin abruptly turns to face me. "You cannot stay. You saw what they did to Dorothea. We have hardly enough to eat and things will just get worse."

I look at the Abbess, fight to speak through my thickened throat. "I cannot leave. Sabiona has been my home, the only safe place I have ever known. It sheltered me when I had nowhere to go. I cannot abandon it—even now."

When I arrived here in 1774, Abbess Mayrin was a new abbess. She knows my story—almost all of it. There is still a part of me that I cannot revisit, let alone lay open to someone else, not even to Abbess Mayrin. I planned to tell her one day, but with every passing year, it has become harder.

"But it is too dangerous to stay alone." Abbess Mayrin's glance turns to my mangled hand. As if to answer, my fingers send out stinging throbs. She is right, I am unable to take care of anything, cannot plant or harvest.

"I will stay with Sister Magdalena." Gertrud's voice is quiet yet determined as she steps in front of us. I have not heard her approach. She kneels and puts her head on Abbess Mayrin's knees. "I beg you, Mother. I cannot leave Magdalena."

And so it is decided. Later today, Abbess Mayrin will take Dorothea away from here. And since Dorothea is too frail to walk, we will place her on a cart the Abbess will pull behind her. It is a difficult journey for a young person, not to mention one of Abbess Mayrin's age. The ground is uneven, often steep up and down.

That's when I realize there may be a way to help Franz.

But in order to move forward, I will need to confess to

the Abbess. And risk her life and his in the process. Not to mention Dorothea's, if she even recovers.

After breakfast, which consists of yesterday's leftover bread and peppermint tea, I make a decision.

The courtyard is buried under more waste, the stench thicker, but I continue my walk past the sleeping soldiers, past guards and wandering and staring men.

The two guards in front of the commander's office stick their bayonets in my direction.

"I must speak with the general," I say, much louder than necessary.

The two guards look at each other, then one of them knocks and disappears inside. In the blink of an eye, he is back, now red-faced and breathing loudly.

"He has no time."

I cross my arms and lean against the wall. "Then I shall wait until he does."

Secretly, I wonder what Abbess Mayrin would say if she knew about my whereabouts… or what I am planning. But if I give up, I might as well sign Franz's death sentence.

The door is ripped open from the inside and bangs against the wall. Out comes a fuming commander, stuffing shirttails into his pants before his gaze finds me.

"I need a word," I say.

"I do not have time for this," he exclaims, but I let his fiery stare bounce off me as if my habit is a giant shield. God must help me now.

"It is but a small request," I say when he makes no move to invite me inside. "Abbess Mayrin will leave today to bring our young sister Dorothea to safety and to a place where she can receive help. She is neither speaking nor eating. Your men…" I take a deep breath. "Never mind. I need a horse or a donkey to draw a cart. Sister Dorothea is not able to walk and we cannot carry her."

The commander looks me up and down. I am pretty sure he understood every word I said, but he seems mute.

"You all leave today," he finally says.

I look at him defiantly. "I will remain with one sister in the guesthouse. You have everything else. I will be growing a garden, so we all have more food."

He abruptly yanks at my sleeve to expose my bluish fingers with the splint. "With that hand?" he mocks.

"I know this land, this earth. I know what it needs and what grows here. If you send a couple of men, we will do better."

My words fade away and silence settles. Above us, somebody shouts, feet trample. The commander's face is unreadable.

"So you want a horse and two men to work the land when you should just leave like the others."

I chew on the inside of my cheek but hold the man's gaze. "This is all I know. I can support you with produce and you can support me… us. It is beneficial for us both."

The commander abruptly turns to one of the guards and says something in rapid French. I think I recognize *cheval*… horse.

When he turns to me, his expression is neutral. He would make a good *bouillotte* player. A long time ago, I watched men play the game in my father's pub. "You tell your Abbess she will have a horse. This afternoon, I shall send two men to help you prepare the garden. At harvest, if there is one, you will give us most."

"Thank you," I manage and quickly lower my head to hide my smile. I am one step closer to getting Franz to safety.

Rushing back to the guesthouse, I realize I have no idea how to smuggle Franz onto the cart in broad daylight. He wears the customary garb of Tirol, a gray felted wool jacket, tight socks and brown knee-length leather pants. I consider looking for a French uniform but dismiss it. Why would a French soldier ride on the cart with two nuns?

Heat creeps up my throat and chokes me. My plan has too many holes.

"What happened?" Gertrud asks when I enter the kitchen.

I shake my head. I will not endanger her any more than necessary.

"Where is Abbess Mayrin?"

"Packing for Sister Dorothea."

I find the Abbess in her room, muttering to herself… "It is God's will, I must trust in Him."

I swallow the dryness in my mouth and say, "May I have a word?"

Abbess Mayrin waves me inside. "We will leave after the midday meal. That allows us to observe the office of *Sext* one last time."

I nod, prayer and food farthest from my mind. "They will give you a horse."

Abbess Mayrin looks at me as if I had spoken perfect French. "How… why?"

"They will give you a horse, so it is easier to travel with Dorothea."

"You spoke with the commander?" Abbess Mayrin's still smooth forehead folds into wrinkles. "When?"

"A little while ago. I knew you would not be able to manage like this."

"I had hoped you would change your mind and help me with her. You and Gertrud would support Dorothea… pull the cart." She pauses. "A horse?" She turns to face me once more, suspicion in her eyes. "What did you tell him… promise him?"

"Nothing, Mother, I told him I would keep the garden and help provide for his soldiers."

"Your hand…"

I nod quickly, the question of Franz heavy on my mind. "We will have help. Two of his men will support us."

"No, no, that cannot be. You are a Benedictine nun, Magdalena, you cannot possibly work alongside the enemy."

"It is the only way for us to stay," I say simply. "I will do what is difficult, because I must."

Abbess Mayrin's eyes are on me… observing as if she sees me for the first time. "You surprise me still, Sister

Magdalena." Then she nods slowly. "Maybe this is what we need to do." She straightens. "Well then, I shall finish packing. Maybe you and Gertrud can prepare Dorothea for the journey?"

My collar is getting tight, so I slide a finger between it and my neck. "Mother, there is one other thing."

Abbess Mayrin sighs. "What is it now, my dear? Have you found a set of wings to fly off this mountain?"

Her attempt at joking fizzles as I try to muster the next words. "Do you remember the men in the sickroom, the boys who fought for the Tirolean army?"

"Of course, they… Sister Gertrud told me about the grave, oh, those poor souls. I have prayed for them."

"It is… there is one, Franz, who is alive."

Once again, Abbess Mayrin stares at me, uncomprehending. "What do you mean?"

"He is hiding in the garden shed. I have been bringing him food and water." Abbess Mayrin opens her mouth to speak, but I rush on. "He will not last much longer and he cannot surrender to the French. They will kill him on the spot."

"What are you thinking?" says Abbess Mayrin very slowly.

Now, Magda, say your piece. "I am wondering if you could take him on the cart, hide him somehow."

Abbess Mayrin jumps from the bed. I have never seen her move this fast. "Sister Magdalena, have you lost your mind? Do you have any idea what will happen if they find him? We will be slain. Even Dorothea, the poor soul. I…"

Until this moment, I have no idea how to get Franz on the cart, but I know it is his only chance. "Please, Mother, he cannot stay. You will only need to get him to the village."

"Past hundreds of French men?"

"It can be done."

"How, Magdalena? How can it be done?"

Here we are, at the crucial question. How indeed will we smuggle the boy off this mountain? "I will find a way," I say aloud. "I must or it will all have been for nothing."

I bow quickly and run from the room. I must think and I must bring Franz food.

Sister Gertrud is kneeling in front of a wooden chest where we keep our old clothes for the poor, the worn-out habits and underclothes, the socks that are shabby… moth-eaten blankets. "I was thinking we would prepare a bed for Dorothea," Gertrud says. "It will be bumpy."

"Abbess Mayrin will receive a horse for our cart." As I glance at the pile of fabric, an idea forms in my head. "Maybe you could help Dorothea get ready, help her wash and put on her clothes?"

Gertrud jumps up and bows respectfully. "Of course, Sister."

Alone in front of the trunk, I quickly begin to rifle through everything. The pile grows until I have what I need.

In the kitchen, I tie the clothes with a piece of cord and attach it under my habit, thanking God for the generous size of my dress. With my good hand, I grab a piece of bread and a small pitcher and slide my sleeve over them.

The air is fresh this morning, sparrows chirp in the laurel hedge that lines the path. Except for the silent sentries along the walls, not too many French are up yet. Head low, I hurry to the shed and close the door behind me.

"Franz?"

There is no sound and I immediately worry, the boy could have done something stupid. But wouldn't I have heard?

"Are you awake?" I ask again.

A grunt comes from the burlap, making me feel equally relieved and anxious. I carefully step closer. It is almost dark back here, but I recognize the bandage that has become filthy.

"I brought you bread," I say, keeping my voice light.

Franz creeps from his hiding spot and the odor of his unwashed body envelopes me like a cloud. "Oh, Sister, I cannot go on. The night was so long." He carefully straightens, and for the first time I realize that he is at least a foot taller than me.

"I have a plan," I say. "There will be a wagon leaving today. Our Abbess is taking a sister away from here."

"Do you imagine the French will allow me to ride along?" Franz's voice is mixture of scorn and resignation. "I cannot even leave this hut without them seeing me."

"That is why I brought you this." I tug at the package beneath my habit and hold it out to him.

"What *is* this?"

"A nun's outfit. Put it on right now. I will take you inside the guesthouse until it is time to leave."

Franz pulls apart the black robes. "I am supposed to put this on?"

"If you want to live, this may be your only chance."

A chuckle rises from the boy's throat. "A nun, hahaha, if my friends could see me now."

"I'll wait. You'd better hurry." With that, I turn my back to him.

Luckily, the habit is long enough to hide Franz's shoes. I place the white veil of the novice over him and instruct him to keep his head low.

From afar, he looks no different than Gertrud—I am hoping the height difference will not be too obvious.

Franz quickly swallows the food I brought before opening the door. All is quiet, so he follows me outside. We have agreed that he will walk behind me. It is easier and he does not have to look up to find his way.

My heart hammers so badly, I feel it in my neck. My ears are on high alert, my eyes dart this way and that, while I try to look downward at the same time. Farther uphill, men's voices mumble. Fifty more yards… thirty.

Only when we arrive in the guesthouse do I remember to breathe. Franz sinks onto a bench in the kitchen. He is panting, which tells me that he is not nearly as recovered as I thought. He may simply die from his injury or from exhaustion—but not on my watch, not if I can help it.

A knock on the door nearly buckles my knees.

"Sister, I have your horse," a voice shouts.

I clear my throat before saying, "One moment, please, I will open the door," well knowing that there is a huge hole gaping where the lock used to be. At the same time, I motion Franz to disappear into the hallway. All I can hope now is that he will not scare the sisters while the French soldier is here.

I carefully open the door a crack and peek outside. A man I have not seen before holds a horse by the reins. "I can help you attach her, if you show me where the cart is," he says. At least that is what I think he says because his German is terrible.

I shake my head. "I can manage." I rush past him, take the mare's bridle, and lead her to a pole in front, hoping that the soldier will follow me. She is a fine horse of a solid brown with white speckles on her flanks. She has been brushed and now sniffs my coif. "Time for a journey," I tell her.

To my annoyance, the soldier hovers. "The commandant wants me to look at your place. We need more room for our soldiers. Now that you are leaving…" He points at the building, obviously intent on following me inside.

Sweat breaks out on my forehead, as I lower my eyes not to show my panic. If Franz has not already startled the sisters, he will certainly be found the minute we step inside.

"I wonder if you might wait until the Abbess leaves," I say. "Sister Dorothea is very scared now, very delicate. She cannot endure seeing… men. She may have a nervous breakdown, even lose her mind."

The man obviously understands better than he speaks because he nods. But when I approach the door, he still stands there. "I will wait until your Abbess leaves."

I struggle to keep my face neutral. "Thank you."

Now I have got a man in a nun's costume I need to smuggle past the eyes of a French guard. It will never work.

As soon as I close the door, I hear voices. In front of Dorothea's room stand a red-faced Abbess and Gertrud, and behind them in the shadows of the hallway looms a tall nun with the beginnings of a scraggly beard.

"What are you thinking?" Abbess Mayrin cries when

she sees me.

"It is the only way," I say quietly, thinking about how I can possibly explain the French man in front of the door or the fact that I envision Franz hiding beneath Dorothea's skirts. "You know what they will do to him."

Gertrud puts a hand on my forearm. "It is too risky."

"They are right," Franz says. He looks so strange in the nun's habit, a gurgle builds in my throat. "I will not risk your lives when you were so kind." His gaze is on me and again I feel the stubbornness rise in me. I must pray and ask forgiveness. Just not now, not when I have an opportunity to save a young life.

I shake my head.

"Even if they did not see his face, they can count," Abbess Mayrin says. "They know we should be four nuns and that two of you are staying." She abruptly grips me by the shoulders. "I want to reason with you. You and Gertrud need to come with us."

Old images rise in my mind: the horrific march to the abbey, climbing in the dark, the cold that engulfed me, the fear of being caught—and the feeling of incredible relief when I gained entry. Meeting Abbess Mayrin for the first time, a woman who did not utter a single word about the state of my dress, who took me in, clothed and fed me when I had nobody and nothing. These walls have protected me for twenty-three years.

"I mean no disrespect, but I cannot go," I say simply. "It is all I know. Who would send notice when the French leave?"

"They may stay here for years," Abbess Mayrin says.

"Surely the war will end one day," I say. "And all those French men will grow uncomfortable to be locked away up here. The French commander has offered help. He will not allow another attack on us."

Doubt shows in the Abbess's eyes, but she remains silent.

"I think you'd better leave soon." Gertrud nods

towards Dorothea, who lies on her bed fully dressed and stares at the ceiling.

"Eh, there is one more thing, actually two." I have to force out the words. "There is a French guard outside… and Franz will need to hide beneath Dorothea's habit."

Incredulity mirrors on Abbess Mayrin's and Gertrud's faces. Even Franz huffs and shakes his head.

"It is impossible," the Abbess says.

"How then will we hide him?" I ask.

"It was a bad idea," Franz says. He looks defeated yet composed. "I will get out of these and surrender."

"No!" I cry. "We can do this. Let me think." Ignoring the mumbles of Abbess Mayrin, I motion Gertrud to follow me. We will need to prepare the cart anyway.

The little two-wheeled wagon we use to transport provisions stands under an overhang at the bottom of the hill. Some larger yard tools, scythes, old furniture, a few baskets and trunks are stacked there. Straw bales from the fall lean against the back. I use them to warm the plants' roots and loosen the soil in early spring, but this year it was forgotten.

I am thankful for the horse walking between us, shielding me from Gertrud's questions. A few years back, we kept a donkey to help turn the earth, but when he passed, we did not replace him. At the time, the abbey did not have enough funds.

The leather of the old breast and hip straps is stiff and cracks in places. I hope it will last long enough to take the three passengers to safety. As I instruct Gertrud how to pull the bellyband underneath the mare, I throw an occasional glance at the French man lingering near the guesthouse.

As I lift straw bales onto the flat cart—I plan to use three so Dorothea can sit comfortably—an idea forms in my head.

I return to the storage area and peruse the old furniture. A trunk would be too obvious, but there is something else that might work. I pull a spider web-covered three-legged milking stool out and inspect it. It might work.

With a grim smile, I motion Gertrud to take a seat on the wagon's bench, take the reins and lead the horse back to the guesthouse. Except the French guard is still there, so I stop for a moment and lean close to Gertrud.

"Will you help me save Franz?" I ask.

Gertrud looks unsure, but as usual, she is on my side. "What is it?"

"I need you to distract the French guard. When we leave the guesthouse, I want you to be somewhere outside and turn your ankle. It is a cheap ruse, but it is all I can think of right now."

Gertrud opens her mouth, but I rush on. "Make sure he faces away from us." I grip her hand with my good one. "Can you promise me that?"

Gertrud nods. "I will remain here, so I can be outside without it being obvious."

"Watch for my sign from the kitchen window," I say before snapping the reins once more.

The guard turns lively as soon as I come to a stop. "I can help with your sister, carry her, perhaps?" There seems to be genuine concern in his expression.

I force a smile. "It is very kind, but we do not want to frighten Sister Dorothea. Thank you for your patience, you can soon inspect inside."

The guard nods and resumes leaning against a tree stump, his gaze casual, but definitely directed toward our house.

Abbess Mayrin sits alone at the table. "I will need help to get Dorothea onto the cart. Where is Sister Gertrud?"

Ignoring the question, I slide next to the Abbess. "I know what to do now. Where is Franz?"

"In one of the rooms. He is weak as well."

"Then we'd better go." I straighten and act confident, but the slightest mishap will expose us all. I find Franz in one of the rooms, lying on his back, motionless.

"Time to leave."

He leans on his elbows and stares at me. "It cannot

work, just leave me be for a few moments."

"You are going. Now. Just help me with Dorothea."

With a sigh, Franz joins me in the hall. Dorothea between us, we guide her into the kitchen. Luckily, she can walk, even if she remains silent.

Abbess Mayrin grips the two small bags and throws me a wary glance.

"Just a second." I step to the window where I quickly rearrange a clay pot. Through the glass, Gertrud meets my eyes and begins to walk toward the guesthouse.

At the front door, I wait and listen and, sure enough, a cry rings out.

"Now," I say and carefully open the door. Outside, the French guard is rushing toward Gertrud, who sits on the ground, her habit a black poufy cloud around her.

I nervously scan the grounds as I guide Dorothea to the cart, where Franz helps her climb onto the platform. I pull apart the straw bales and place the milking stool into the opening. My heart hammers fiercely as I wave Franz to me and motion him to climb into the hole. He frowns but knows better than to question me now. Head and knees toward the bench, he folds himself around the stool. Dorothea still stands dreamily on the cart, so I make her sit on the stool, her back facing the bench.

"Hand me the bags and get on the bench," I say to Abbess Mayrin, who waits open-mouthed next to the cart. While the Abbess laboriously climbs on top, I drape Dorothea's habit over the stool and Franz, set the two bags on either side of her on the straw. Now it looks as if Dorothea sits on a straw bale herself. I do not want to imagine how cramped Franz must be, but he will have to endure. In the distance, Gertrud moans. The French man kneels next to her and inspects her ankle. Gertrud has made sure that her habit chastely covers her legs.

I climb down and raise a hand to Abbess Mayrin. "Go with God." Then, in a whisper, "Let him out down in the village. He will find his way."

"You are a brave soul, Sister Magdalena," Abbess Mayrin says. "I will pray for you."

Our eyes meet one last time before the Abbess snaps the reins and the cart slowly rumbles toward the gate. *Please, dear Lord, let them be safe, let them travel off this mountain and let Franz find his family.*

The next minutes refuse to pass. I want to wave, want to run with them, make sure they pass through the gates, maybe distract the guards, cry, sing or shout. Instead, as I make my way to Sister Gertrud, I strain to hear past my coif, past the veil, past the main house and courtyard, I listen for sounds, shots or screams or some kind of distress.

All I hear is the low voice of Sister Gertrud and the deep one of the French soldier.

"What happened?" I ask, putting some irritation into my voice.

"I twisted my foot." Gertrud looks up at me, relief written in her eyes. "This man is trying to help." In the morning light, her skin is flawless against the white coif and veil, her eyes as blue as the sky above. No wonder the French soldier cannot take his gaze off her.

"Maybe you could help her get up?" I ask the man, who hardly pays attention to me. Still, I listen to the sounds beyond the wall.

Nothing.

Gertrud places a hand on the man's forearm, and he picks her up and sets her on her feet as if she were a feather. She leans heavily on him before taking my hand.

"I think I can manage," she says with a weak smile. "Thank you for your kindness. Sister Magdalena will help me inside."

The French soldier tips his hat and I have the distinct feeling he wishes me far away.

When the man turns, he opens his mouth in surprise. Somehow, he has missed the Abbess leaving, has missed my ruse.

"Perhaps you want to inspect the guesthouse now?" I

ask, making sure my smile is mild.

CHAPTER TWELVE

Fall/Winter 1797

Twenty-four soldiers have joined us in the guesthouse—Gertrud and I share a cell once more. It is almost impossible to pray, the building noisy with shouting and trampling feet. How can men be so loud and so foul smelling?

Gertrud, whose ankle miraculously healed overnight, and I are trying to stay out of the way. We spend most of our time outdoors, walking the paths or taking refuge in the old church. But even here it is hardly quiet. At any moment, soldiers barge in, walk with their dirty boots on the holy ground, talk loudly while we are attempting to pray.

Our Jesus statue has disappeared. I think grimly about the pieces I have hidden away in a secret compartment beneath a stone tile.

I wonder what Benedict would say if he could see us now. Two soldiers help in the garden. My hand has almost healed, the fingers no longer so swollen, but holding tools is still painful and I have little control of ring and little finger. I suspect some bone in there did not grow back together well.

The men are at work, digging, trenching, watering and harvesting. Both keep their eyes on Gertrud, who pretends not to notice. Especially the French man who brought the horse often seeks her proximity, tries to make her laugh. Sometimes,

I hear Gertrud's giggle as well, a strange sound on this holy mountain. I worry I may have started something between them. Until now, I thought Gertrud immune to such human feelings, but I am not so sure anymore. I do not know her history, it is something only Abbess Mayrin is familiar with.

I so hope for some post from the Abbess—it has been five months. Has she arrived at the bishop's summer residence? Is Franz safe? The land continues to war, though there has been word of a peace agreement between Austria and France. We now have an official truce, but the French are still here. If anything, they are wilder and louder, constantly search for entertainment. They have created a bocce field, the former grass now trampled and dead, surrounded by rubbish.

Most of the grapes along the mountain have been ravaged, either eaten or taken to make wine. Only these French men do not understand how to do it properly and I am not about to show them.

Today I am picking the last grapes, a variety with small berries, but sweet as sugar. Setting down the basket to wipe my sweaty forehead, I hear a shout.

Near the wall, a French guard sags forward and then slides to the ground. My ears detect a pop and not thirty feet away along the wall, another French man sinks to the ground, then another.

I call to Sister Gertrud, who is on her knees, pulling weeds, "Something is happening."

Shouts erupt near the main house, while I am trying to decide what to do. I want to be able to watch, but we must be safe at the same time.

"Who is shooting?" Gertrud asks as soon as she reaches me. Her habit has dirt stains where her knees are.

"I cannot see anything," I say. "You do not suppose the Tiroleans are back to free us?"

But while new French guards take posts along the wall, the shots cease.

And then I understand. Tirol only made advances because the men are trained sharpshooters. In this mountainous region, they sneak closer and then pick off the French.

Near the main house, the commandant is shouting orders. Groups of soldiers line up and then march off, no doubt in search of the attackers.

I grin. They will not find them. This is neither their land nor do they understand the terrain. I know I should not feel pleasure when men kill each other. But this occupation is pushing us to the limit.

All winter it is quiet. I had so hoped for an attack to rid ourselves of the French, but other than occasional sniper shots, nothing is happening. Our fall crops were glorious, but most of them have already been consumed, and Sister Gertrud and I must manage on minimal rations.

The cold is terrible. Normally we received wood from the villagers who generously transported wagons with logs here. Since the French arrived, no villager will come near. Who could blame them? I am wearing two tunics to keep out some of the icy air. I cannot even go outside, the ground is frozen and covered under snow.

At night, Gertrud and I tremble under the covers. We are sharing a bed to keep each other a bit warmer, but even our room feels frozen. Ice blooms cover the windows, frost grows on the blanket in front of our mouths.

The cold paired with the constant gnawing in my middle is wearing me down. I force my mind to other matters to distract myself. Abbess Mayrin sent word that she and Dorothea are staying with a family, that she had "stopped" in the village of Klausen to check on the old harness. I take it as her way to tell me that Franz has made it to safety. This fact alone keeps me going. Gertrud and I no longer go to pray in our churches. It feels perilous with so many men about, especially for my young and beautiful sister. Worse is how lonely we feel.

Doubt has become my companion. Doubt about the wisdom of staying here and forcing Gertrud to share our plight. At the bishop's summer residence, we would be in the company of our sisters. We could pray and live the Benedictine way in our community. Yes, we would be guests, but would that be so bad? What am I doing here among strangers?

As spring returns, the sniper shots increase again, especially since the first green provides better cover.

It makes the French fidget. They no longer stand in the open along the walls to watch over the land because the shots come out of nowhere at all times of day, even at night when there is a moon. There is no pattern to it, no rule, except for one: make every shot count. The Tirolian sharpshooters manage it all the time.

Dozens of French soldiers have been injured or killed. Quite often their wounds fester and the men succumb after months. It is cruel and I should feel mercy, feel compassion, pray for the suffering, and yet... I cannot find the strength. All I pray for are the Tiroleans and that they find more targets and rescue us.

The guesthouse, our last refuge, is not equipped to house many people, its stove in the kitchen hardly large enough to warm the space.

Most of the time, Gertrud and I are hiding in our cell because the French are antsy and look for distraction. Several have made advances toward Gertrud. They poke fun at our ways, our praying.

A knock pulls me from my thoughts. Sister Gertrud and I exchange frightened glances, and before I can say something, the door is torn open.

One of the soldiers who is staying here motions us to come along.

I realize it has been a year since the French first arrived. Our beloved abbey is almost unrecognizable, the filth and stench unbearable. How will we make it through another summer when the temperatures broil the air and turn this mountain into a cesspool?

The grass has been trampled and has died, replaced by

mud and garbage. The stench of excrement and urine is now so strong, I want to bury my nose. Much of our furniture not essential for sleeping or eating has been burned for warmth—even the church pews. My heart cries as we follow the French soldier to the main house.

Gertrud and I never venture here, there are too many unnerved and bored men spoiling for entertainment. I recognize the hallway to the office of Abbess Mayrin, the place I pleaded with the commandant. I have not spoken to him since I asked for the horse.

"In here," the soldier says, half shoving us into the office. Abbess Mayrin's refuge has been plundered as well. The floor planks are covered in mud and the wood I see beneath is scraped, the seating arrangement near the window missing. Maps I do not recognize cover walls and desk. A likeness of Napoleon has replaced the picture of Saint Benedict.

"What is the meaning of this?" The commandant steps from the shadows. I hardly recognize him because his chin is hidden under a mangle of beard.

Gertrud and I look at each other. "What is it you are asking?" I say.

The commander throws up his arms. "This, this… slaughter?"

I stare at the French man. *Was it not him who spoke of war? Is he not the one occupying a place that is not his to claim?* "I do not understand."

"What do you know about the sharpshooters?"

Again, I stare. "I know nothing… we are prisoners here in our own home." I clamp shut my mouth, knowing I do not want to goad this obviously desperate man.

"You know nothing?" The commander falls into the chair and leans back, his dark eyes on us.

"As I said—"

"Let the young one speak," the commandant barks.

Gertrud lowers her gaze. I know she is frightened, feel her trembling next to me.

"Look at me, woman."

Gertrud reluctantly lifts her gaze. "I... know... nothing."

Abruptly, the commandant pounds a fist on the papers, then rises. Some scatter and fall to the floor. "Of course, how could I forget?" he mocks. "You are married to God. All you do is pray." He is red in the face and I brace myself for the worst.

But the blow never comes. Instead, he towers above, one forefinger pokes at us. "I tell you what you will do, as of now, you will help take care of the injured."

Without waiting for our reply, he shouts something and the guard from earlier roughly grips my arm.

They march us toward the sick quarters that have been expanded to additional rooms, because there are so many injured. I keep my head low. On the one hand, I want to smile because I can tell that the French commander is truly desperate. Sitting up here on this holy mountain is not what a soldier does. And on top of that, his men are being killed by an unseen enemy.

At the same time, I cringe because everything inside of me wants to refuse the new task. Gertrud and I find ourselves inside, every available inch covered with beds and on them suffering and dying men. The air is unbelievably foul, so foul, I am choking and have to close my eyes. *Please, Lord, give me strength.* In addition to the odors outside, the most otherworldly smells humanity can produce cling to me. The men are filthy, the beds too and the floor is covered with everything from dried pus to vomit.

Next to me, Gertrud heaves. Maybe it is best if we have little to eat. It would certainly make its way back up.

Patting Gertrud on the arm, I announce loudly, "We need fresh water and soap."

One of the men guarding the door appears to understand and soon several buckets with water appear. At least they have not fouled it up yet or we would all have to leave.

"I will wash the men," I tell Gertrud. "You clean the

beds."

And so it begins, a new trial of caring for the unfortunate—God is surely testing us.

CHAPTER THIRTEEN

I have been careful not to speak to the French too much. I do not want to get attached, find another Franz I must worry about. It would be easy because most of these wretches are just young men who used to live in another country and whose ruler has ordered them to fight and kill.

It is unfortunate how governments constantly use their citizens for their own foolish gain. What makes this man, Napoleon Bonaparte, so bloodthirsty, so megalomaniacal to think he should take over the world? Why does he think he needs to occupy an abbey in the middle of Tirol? It is madness, and yet we are powerless. These men are powerless as well, they follow orders. And if they refuse, they are shot for desertion or treason.

The men are mostly thankful, those who still are in their right mind. Some are so feverish, they burn from the wounds that turn black and fester and then, as the blackness creeps up their limbs, the stench of the dying flesh becomes unbearable. Their doctor has apparently left to help out farther south, so there is nobody to support Gertrud and me.

I have been using Hildegard von Bingen's recipes to treat abscesses and oozing wounds with vervain compresses, fever with tincture of columbine, wash the men's scabies-reddened skin with mint-infused water. Some French respond well, others just wither and die. I pray for them, but my heart is not in it. So, I pray for compassion, for understanding and patience.

We could work around the clock and still never have enough time to take care of everyone. Many of the injured cannot eat by themselves and feeding and cleaning them takes time. Newly injured men join us every day and the sick bay has expanded to a third room.

I am just pouring out a bucket of bloodied water from a young man who was shot in the shoulder this morning when I hear the unmistakable sound of shots. This time, there are many and they come from beyond the walls. The Tiroleans are back!

The guards have long disappeared since we began working here, so I fetch Gertrud and together we rush back to the guesthouse. It is empty except for the usual utter devastation of our kitchen. Cups and plates cover tables and shelves, dirty pots sit in front of the fire. Ever since Gertrud and I started spending all day in the infirmary, we have no more time to clean here.

"What is happening?" Gertrud asks as we clear a spot at the table.

"I think our rescue is finally here."

"What can we do?"

Gertrud's simple question echoes through my mind. What indeed? And then it comes to me. "I will return soon."

"What are you going to do?"

I shake my head. "Promise me you'll stay here." After a look at Gertrud's young face, I add, "Best if you hide in our cell. Push my bed in front of the door."

"Please stay." Gertrud attempts to grip my sleeve, but I am faster.

"I must help," I say. "It is best if you do not know…"

"Magdalena…"

Closing the door snuffs out Gertrud's voice. I hesitate, urge my ears to pick up sounds. There is definitely an attack going on. I sneak outside. Along the wall that overlooks the path, French soldiers line up, shooting and reloading. The garden is quiet, so I hurry toward it, then the shed. The memory of Franz hits me, as I step inside to catch my breath. If I get caught, I will die. At least it is for something I believe in.

I creep back outside and around the shed. Behind it, stone steps lead to a small gate. It is hidden between bushes that are now overgrown with honeysuckle and ivy. We used to take this shortcut to visit the Church of Our Lady on the other side, many locals would make pilgrimages there when it was still safe. It is located at the lowest point of the abbey and can be reached from the public trail.

I listen and take a look around. Nothing. From here, I cannot see the wall or the main buildings, not even the guesthouse. If I am asked, I could pretend to visit the church. The gate's lock is rusty as I turn the key, its hinges creak.

Ever so slowly, I step through. Nobody is down here, no French and no Tiroleans, the sounds of gunfire muffled. Unsure about what to do next, I head for the church. My back tingles as if somebody is watching and I resist the urge to turn around. If there are sharpshooters, they can pick me off easily.

As my fingers cramp around the old key, the knuckles of my ring finger protest. My hand has not been the same since the French soldier stepped on it. Our Lady is silent and when I walk toward the altar, it is almost as if she is holding her breath—along with me.

The familiar scent of incense tickles my nose. I kneel in the front pew and lower my head. Maybe God will guide Tirol's sharpshooters to locate lots of French soldiers. Maybe they will find the hidden door.

I must pray for forgiveness for my thoughts of fury toward Napoleon's men. Did they not disrupt my vows of constancy, the promise to remain with one community? How does it agree with obedience, the second vow I took when I became a Benedictine nun? We are to honor a human's decency and individuality. Does it apply to warring French men?

I have no answers and, like so often lately, God refuses to answer. Only Benedict's last vow, that of living simply and without splendor, in fact ascetic, do we follow well. Actually, too well. I have lost so much weight, my habit appears even roomier than before. I am not nearly as strong either.

I pause in my thoughts. Did the door just click shut? I sense a presence more than I hear it. None of my senses appear to work, our Lady is as silent as our Lord.

I will return to my post now and leave the door unlocked. God may lead the Tirolean sharpshooters—

"Sister?"

I turn so abruptly, my veil flies and momentarily covers my eyes. I swipe it aside and am face to face with a man in a wool sweater, knee-length leather pants and the traditional felt hat most natives wear. His brownish beard is so thick, his mouth is invisible. But even in the gloom of the church, his eyes shine like two distant stars.

"I did not mean to startle you." The man's voice is deep and as throaty as if he is fighting a cold. "How are you managing?"

I look at the man, momentarily mute. When has anybody asked me how *I* was doing? Nobody ever cared enough to find out. "Eh, I… we are holding up. Just barely, though, food is sparse and the French are nervous."

A chuckle rises from the beard. "They will be gone soon."

I nod and, in this moment, I feel the urge to hug this stranger. *Quit being silly*, the voice in my head comments. But I must have smiled because the man asks, "That is cause for happiness?"

"Yes," I say quietly. "It is a great relief to have your men near." A long time ago, I resented the country's Tiroleans coming here. Now I cannot wait to see them move back. At least they are God-fearing, even if their habits grate on me—

"…down here?"

I feel the eyes of the man on me, realize I have not heard him. "What?"

"I asked how you got down here. Surely you did not wander through the main entrance out in the open."

This time, I smile with purpose. "There is a small gate hidden near here. We sisters used to come this way when—"

"You mean we have a way inside?" The man's beard trembles as he speaks.

"Just watch me carefully. I will leave it unlocked. Sister Gertrud and I are in the guesthouse near the gardens. We are the only ones left. I'd better go now."

"How many men are there?"

"Four hundred to start. There are fewer now… some have moved on, you picked off others last fall and a few dozen have died."

The man bows respectfully and lets me pass. "God bless you, Sister."

"I will pray for you."

I can hardly contain myself, want to tell Sister Gertrud about our good fortune, but when I come up the path behind the gardening shed, I hear voices. Sure enough, ten or fifteen French soldiers are standing not thirty feet away. Even though I understand little French—I have picked up words in the infirmary—I know they are arguing, their voices loud and aggressive—maybe fearful.

I creep behind the shed and sink to my knees. If I could get *into* the shed, I might pretend to have spent time in there. But the door is on the other side and there is not even a window on this end. If I show myself now, they may wonder where I came from and discover the secret door in the wall.

How long will it take before the Tiroleans slip inside? I must be gone by then or the French will know what I did and kill Gertrud and me.

From some place near the main house comes an explosion. It is so violent, the ground shakes. It also wakes up the French men who scatter, some running toward the noise, others toward the wall.

I slip past the hut and follow the path to our

guesthouse.

Our cell's door is open, our beds inside helter-skelter. Somebody must have gone through the contents because bedding and our few belongings, even our bibles, are on the floor.

Gertrud! Fear like I have never felt before grips me. It is so strong, I can hardly force my body to move. But I must or Gertrud…

I call for her as I rush back outside. The air, grown acrid with gun smoke, chokes me, but I cannot let that stop me. A few soldiers rush past, ignore me.

My feet urge me forward and when I find myself in the corridor to Abbess Mayrin's office, I know what I need to do. Instead of the two guards, there is just one to stop me.

"I need to speak with the commandant."

Recognizing me, he calls something through the door which is ripped open a moment later. A hand grips my arm and pulls me inside. There sits Gertrud and the momentary relief makes me sigh. But the commandant is shouting at me. "Where were you?"

I stare at Gertrud's red-rimmed eyes, her fidgeting hands. The commander apparently interrogated her. He is looking for a scapegoat instead of helping his men.

The man's fingers squeeze harder. "I asked where you were?"

I lower my head. "I went to pray."

"Where?"

"The old church."

"On top of the hill?"

"Yes."

"You are lying! We searched for you. I have been suspicious of you for a while, *Sister*." He almost spits the last word. "It was a mistake to allow you to remain."

You shall not lie. I want to shout at the man, tell him what I did. But that would endanger our rescue. So, I just shake my head. "All I did was pray."

"Why did you leave your sister then, leave her

barricaded in her room?" The commandant's brows are so low, his eyes lie in shadow. "Is that your last word?"

I say nothing, but for once I keep my gaze on the man's face. It is a mistake because he must have read my defiance. My mother used to say that she could read my expression like a book.

Sure enough, he shouts, "You treasonous witch, you shall die."

Gertrud cries something unintelligible as a terrible sense of doom engulfs me.

But there is no time to think, not even to pray for wisdom. The commandant bellows to his guard, rough hands grip me and I am led outside like a sheep to slaughter.

Behind me, Gertrud pleads, "Please, dear sir, she has done nothing wrong. She has helped your men survive with her garden. She has treated your sick with her medicine. She is a nun, married to God."

But the commander does not seem to hear because suddenly, Gertrud's voice fades and he is next to me. Together we hurry through the corridor into the garden, my haven.

I am numb inside, see myself walking along while my soul already flies above. I will join God sooner than expected, but I have no fear. Only the worry about Gertrud burns inside me, and a feeling I had long believed forgotten: white-hot hatred.

I struggle to prepare myself, do not want to face God in such a state. I must be calm and forgiving. Even now.

Right—I cannot.

"Stand against the wall," the commandant barks. "Or I will make you." He nods at the guard, who leaves, undoubtedly returning to Gertrud. There is no telling what they will do to her now.

I do as I am told, lean back against the stone, still warm from the sun. The firmness of the abbey supports me. Behind me, the warring appears to continue unabated. Men shout, shots rain as numerous as hail, but they all fade.

I have a view of the garden, where the first shoots have

broken through the earth. This time, I will not see them bear fruit.

The commandant has pulled out his pistol, a heavy thing with a wooden handle he now points at me.

"Please allow me a last prayer," I say. I am surprised how firm my voice sounds. I am proud of that voice.

The man mumbles something like, "Hurry up."

I lift my head toward the sky, lift my hands, palms up to ask God for forgiveness, ask him to welcome me.

"Enough!" The commandant's pistol points at me and even though I do not want to, I look at it, at him, a man who is killing a nun. I have trouble focusing. The commandant's features wiggle and grow vague. Is my soul already leaving?

A shot rings out, I flinch. My mind checks for injuries, but I feel no pain. The commandant missed me. But then he stumbles and the pistol sinks to his side, then drops to the ground. On his chest is a tiny hole which now fills with blood, spreads across the fabric of his vest, outward… faster. I stand there, try to comprehend what has happened, when a man in an Austrian felt hat rushes to my side.

"Sister Magdalena!" he cries, out of breath and joyful at the same time.

Now I am glad for the wall behind me, because I need it to hold me steady. The man's features are hidden under a heavy beard. He wears a black eye patch. "Do you not recognize me? It is Franz."

"Franz," is all I say, extending an arm to his cheek. "You are so… grown."

He smiles and gently takes me by the elbow. "You'd better hide until this is over."

Now I see other Tiroleans swarm through the garden. They have appeared out of nowhere from behind the shed.

When Franz wants to lead me to the guesthouse, I suddenly stop. "I must find Gertrud. She was in the French commandant's office."

"I will find her." Franz gently but firmly pushes me toward the entry. "I promise." He smiles at me, a real smile.

"We will get rid of them, all of them."

All evening and through the night, the Tiroleans sweep the abbey to find the last hideouts of French soldiers, whom they take prisoner and march them off the mountain.

Gertrud and I are sitting inside the guesthouse, eating bread and drinking peppermint tea. Even if we did have supplies, neither of us is in the mood to cook. Though I should feel joyous, the scene of my near-execution replays in my head. It is true, I felt ready to join God, but I prefer to remain here on earth a bit longer. Sabiona needs me. Especially now. Gertrud stares at the wall, the silence between us comfortable and yet heavy. The ordeal we went through, the daily fight for survival, is taking its toll.

In the morning, I walk to the well. My body feels as if it is filled with rocks and though I urge on my feet, I can muster no more than a shuffle. I vow to rest today, just help Gertrud clean our kitchen.

"Look who we have here."

I have not allowed myself to think about the man who abused me so long ago, but I would recognize Georg anywhere. I turn slowly to face him. I am so tired, the words refuse to form in my head.

Despite his words, Georg looks terrible. His eyes are bloodshot, the skin on his face is sallow and gray, blood seeps through the bandage on his right hand. "Are you mute, all of a sudden? I thought you nuns talk all the time." He chuckles, but underneath I detect something else, maybe a worry or uncertainty.

I want to turn away, tell him to leave me alone, but all I do is stand there. That quiet inactivity seems to confuse him further. All I do is look at him, study him. And in that moment, I realize I am not afraid anymore. I just stand there and watch my former tormentor.

Georg moves closer until less than two feet remain. He smells rotten, his clothes are dirty beyond repair.

"You look old, sister."

I am sure I do, but it matters not. Benedict's teachings are more important than earthly vanity. Besides, I have earned the right to look old. I smile.

"Speak, woman, speak."

I take a deep breath. "Oh, Georg, what could we possibly talk about?" I turn my back to him and continue to the well. I half expect him to follow me, keep pestering and threatening, but all remains quiet. As I work the chain and fill my bucket, I notice Georg still standing where I left him.

He appears forlorn, kind of lost, the subject of his desire and his scorn has turned her back on him. He throws a glance toward me, then turns and slowly wanders toward the main house. Again, I smile, but then the bucket blurs as a rattled sigh leaves my throat.

It is over.

PART II
CHAPTER FOURTEEN

Sabiona Abbey, 1808

I am sitting in the shade of an apple tree and fan myself. The August sun scorches from a cloudless sky and the usual wind is absent today. Our black habits and veils are not too suitable for garden work in the heat. Thankfully, Gertrud is strong and our new novice, Sister Benedikta, is helping. Right now, they are carrying water buckets to keep our tomatoes and peppers happy.

"How are you holding up?" Abbess Mayrin sinks heavily onto the bench next to me, a cane by her side. Her formerly smooth forehead is deeply grooved and lines around her mouth cut toward her chin. She has just turned eighty and the burdens of leading the abbey have left their mark.

"Hot but pleased," I say simply. "My gardens are finally back to their old glory." Indeed, our cellars and stores are filled again. It has taken nearly ten years to clean and repair, to scrub Sabiona of the filth left by the French.

After that fateful day I expected to die, Franz and his sharpshooters saved not only me, but more importantly restored the abbey. And though Georg remained at Sabiona for weeks, after that fateful encounter by the well, he never spoke to me again. That winter, Abbess Mayrin and my sisters returned and together we have been rebuilding ever since.

There were many days when I thought I would simply lie down and give up. Especially in the first weeks when the extent of the damage became clear. Every room, every window, every piece of bedding, furniture and inch of floor had to be scoured. The outside was as bad, if not worse. The smell of urine and excrement lingered for two years. We reseeded grass and flowers, straightened vineyard and gardens. We cleansed each church from top to bottom, often worked extra shifts after dinner service. Many sculptures, books and invaluable relics went missing.

The understanding Father Schweiggl had with the first group of French did not last long. We emptied our last savings for nothing. Had it not been for the generosity of the surrounding villagers, we would not have survived.

Each prayer and service gave me strength, but I did not think we would ever get done. And yet here we are.

Abbess Mayrin nods but remains serious. "I am worried about more unrest. Bonaparte is emperor and we supposedly belong to Bavaria's kingdom now because they allied with France." A deep sigh heaves from Abbess Mayrin's chest. "I cannot believe they forbade the ringing of church bells."

We are still using our bell to call to prayer, but have to abstain from Sunday services. The villagers are not allowed to visit, though some do it secretly. Yearly processions at Easter and Christmas have been canceled. The families in Tirol are deeply unhappy about these new laws—God and worship have accompanied them from the crib to the grave. Now all of a sudden it is a crime to attend church? It is wrong.

"…they leave."

I turn toward the Abbess, recognize her shriveled hand on my sleeve. I have not heard a word. "I am sorry, Mother."

She gives a tiny nod and says, "I wonder if those dreadful French will ever leave this land. First they ruined our abbey, now the Bavarians are working with them. Napoleon handed Tirol to the Bavarians as a gift."

It wasn't theirs to give. "One would think they would grow tired of living in a foreign land, committing crimes…"

"Some men thrive from the power of it."

Indeed, some men crave power over everything else and many still claim to do God's work… take what they please and force the weak under their will. What bible do they read? Which part did I miss?

The bell rings and I help Abbess Mayrin to her feet. Together we make our way to *None*, our afternoon prayer. The walls of the abbey church welcome me, the air in here is cool and still. Immediately, I sink into my space, turn inward to that peaceful place where I converse with God.

I cannot say if I am content with the way he is overseeing our land. The young men of Tirol are now being conscripted by Bavaria… they are supposed to fight for the enemy. I think of the many who lost their lives, Franz who barely got away from the French army, and now is considered an ally of the French? How can God watch this mayhem and not intervene?

Young Benedikta's clear voice rises to the heavens. She stands up front and despite the coolness in here, her cheeks glow. She is shy and speaks in a quiet voice. Only when she sings does she forget her nervousness. Like most of us, she has her reasons to be here. Like so many of us, she keeps them to herself. As confessor, Father Schweiggl listened to many of our stories. He left four years ago and never heard mine. Something in the way he spoke bothered me, a lurking in his gaze I never warmed to. And while he meant well to keep the French at bay, in the end it did not work. We scraped together payment, signed a contract that was soon forgotten.

I look up in surprise as the nuns around me rise. I vow to pay better attention when the door to the church is opened from the outside. I am in back, closest to the exit and get a good view of the man in a soldier's uniform, the tall gold-ornamented hat, the fancy jacket and gray pants. At first, I think it is a French soldier, but then I recognize him for what he is: a Bavarian infantryman.

Shrieks and cries erupt around me, but all I do is stand there and stare. A terrible foreboding broils up inside me, and I am glad the habit hides my shaking limbs.

"Where is your Abbess?" the man says. He is young, in his early twenties, the strap of his enormous hat hides a certain weakness in his features.

"Right here," Abbess Mayrin says behind me. I step aside and together we approach the man.

He pulls a letter from a leather pouch and hands it to the Abbess. "Your abbey is being abolished. You should leave immediately."

As the words *abolished* and *leave* echo through my mind, I concentrate on the paper in the Abbess's hand. It is shaking so badly, I cannot make out any words. Only the white- and blue-checkered crest glows.

Abbess Mayrin hands me the paper. "You read it… my eyes."

"In acknowledgment of the state of Bavaria's secularization efforts, the standing of Sabiona Abbey is revoked with immediate effect. All worldly goods and materials of value are to be confiscated by representatives of the Royal Bavarian Army and liquidated at their earliest convenience. The occupants of Sabiona are to leave the premises immediately."

"You cannot do that!" I shout. The paper has taken on a life of its own as I wave it in the man's face. He is hardly taller than I, but I can tell I surprised him because he takes a step back. In the man's expression, incredulity turns into anger.

"You'd better watch out, Sister," he huffs. "It is the king's order."

Whose king, I want to shout. But I say nothing as the teachings of Benedict, God and Mother Mary tumble through my mind and collide with my fury. I am once again helpless.

Abbess Mayrin limps to my side and takes my hand. But not even she can utter a response.

"See that your convent leaves by tomorrow." The young man marches off and leaves the doors standing wide open. Outside, he throws up his arms as he walks toward a group of fellow soldiers. They are here to kick us out… again. Just like that, Sabiona Abbey is no more.

Instead of joyful prayers and song, mumbles and sniffles fill the church, rise up to the heavens. Oh, God, what is happening?

Tears creep into my eyes, the cross in front blurs until Jesus is no more than a shadow. I blink hard, clear my vision, do not care about the wetness on my cheeks. I am done being strong. I cannot cope any longer. All our struggles have been in vain.

"What will we do?" Gertrud says. The trials of our lives have aged her, but she is still beautiful despite the lines around her eyes and mouth. When I ran away more than thirty years ago, I had wanted to find a new home. Sabiona gave that to me. My sisters and Abbess Mayrin replaced my family, stood by my side, never questioned my actions.

Only Abbess Mayrin knows what happened. And she has never uttered a word about it since, refused to even acknowledge my questions.

"Where should we go?" Gertrud's face is so close, I notice the tiny freckles on her nose. I can tell she wants me to stay. Like last time, when she remained by my side in spite of four hundred French soldiers.

I try for a smile, fail and sigh instead. "We must talk it through… together." Abbess Mayrin has slumped into a pew, surrounded by several other nuns. Our numbers have shrunken to less than forty, but there are Adelheid—Augusta passed into the Lord's arms last year—even Dorothea. After her ordeal with the French soldiers, she did not speak for two years, and her hair, that beautiful copper color, turned a mottled gray—I only know this because I helped take care of Dorothea during a bout of influenza.

Even now, her voice is so quiet, one has to lean in to make out her words. Abbess Mayrin excused her from singing or reciting in front and has taken care of her ever since they left together on that cart. The two of them are close even now.

Maybe Dorothea is the daughter the Abbess never had. I worry what will happen when Abbess Mayrin leaves us.

By the time we file out of church, the walkways and courtyard swarm with Bavarian soldiers. We hurry past, heads low, intent on getting to our cells. I had planned to spend the rest of the afternoon in the garden, but there are more important matters. Already, the intruders swarm through our innermost sanctum as if they own it.

In the main house, I turn down the corridor past the Abbess's office into the library. Terrible memories intrude as I step inside. I used to come here in the winter to study, but ever since Dorothea's misfortune, I cannot bear to be here. Now I must. There are thousands of invaluable letters, scrolls, diaries and books that may fall prey to the Bavarians.

Where should I hide them?

"Where are you going?" Gertrud catches up to me.

"I will save the archives," I say quietly.

Gertrud nods. "Let me fetch a few trunks from the attic."

Only now do I realize that I had no good plan on how to transport the books. Gertrud is right, so I say, "Excellent, I will go with you."

For the rest of the afternoon, we pack the old trunks with the history of Sabiona. Luckily, not too many men are inside. Benedikta and another novice have joined us and by evening, the shelves are empty, trunks stacked against the wall. Now it looks as if we are packing for our journey.

"Where to?" Gertrud asks. "We cannot possibly take all these things with us."

"I have a place," I whisper. "Let us move them after dark."

As we assemble for dinner, I notice carts and wagons lined up in the courtyard. At first, I think they may be for our journey. But then I see the men carrying armfuls of candleholders, cups, monstrances, crosses, sculptures, paintings and tapestries. After the French and Tiroleans left, we had restocked our altars and places of respite, never expecting another attack.

How could I have been so naïve? My stomach roils as I see the wagons fill with the heart of our abbey.

"They are stealing everything," Gertrud shrieks.

At that moment, two men carry a golden chest that contains the holy sacraments used during mass past us. I lunge forward and tug at the corner. The men let go; apparently I surprised them. I hug the chest to me. "It is ours," I shout. "Such cruelty cannot be the king's wish!"

The two soldiers say nothing, just stand there and look at me. Is that embarrassment in their eyes? I swiftly turn and march off toward the main house, Gertrud running after me.

Only when we enter Abbess Mayrin's office do my arms begin to tremble.

"What are you doing with our chest?" Abbess Mayrin asks with mild surprise. She looks especially tired, kind of shrunken.

"Sister Magdalena took it from the men," Gertrud says. "They are robbing us."

For a moment, the room sinks into silence. I am still hugging the chest, one corner digs into my stomach. I slightly adjust the load and then carefully set it on the desk in front of our Abbess.

"I could not let them take our holiest relic."

"Oh, my child, they could have hurt you," Abbess Mayrin says.

"I do not care for my safety," I say heatedly. What does it matter if Sabiona is gone? But then I realize my tone and add, "I am sorry, Mother. It is unjust and I want to help."

"Have you decided where you want to go?" she asks.

A knock at the door makes us freeze. Without waiting for an answer, a man struts into the office.

"You the Abbess, I presume?" His accent is from the deep south of Bavaria. He is tall and meaty, a strong muscled man in his thirties with thick hands and a reddish complexion.

Our Mother looks resigned. "I am Abbess Mayrin, how may I help you?"

"Your nuns, eh, sorry, I mean, Corporal Maier at your service." He kicks his heels together and I am wondering, for the first time, if some of those men have retained a bit of upbringing, some morals or a conscience. "I have orders to assist you."

How, I want to ask, but Abbess Mayrin is faster. She may have a quiet voice now, one softened by age, but right now, she sounds as sharp as my best kitchen knife. "How could you possibly assist us, Corporal?"

"Your younger nuns, they are to become teachers at some of the remaining cloisters which have been made into boarding schools." His eyes wander to Gertrud, whose power of beauty still remains. "How many nuns under forty or fifty do you have?"

Abbess Mayrin mumbles something before her gaze meets that of the soldier. "I doubt that our sisters would like to educate children. They came here to be close to God, to follow Saint Benedict's teachings. They were not hurting anyone… until you arrived."

"It is by the order of King Maximilian I of Bavaria."

Abbess Mayrin leans back. "I only answer to one king, and he is up there." Her gaze flicks to the ceiling and right back. In that moment, I feel intense pride for our Mother who has taken care of our abbey and us for decades.

Since the corporal momentarily seems to have lost his speech, Abbess Mayrin continues. "I am not quite clear… why did *your* king decide to secularize Sabiona? He could not possibly be bothered by our quiet ways and we surely have no worldly goods he would covet."

Corporal Maier clears his throat, his cheeks aflame. "I was told it is too expensive to feed so many people?"

Abbess Mayrin stares. "Thirty-eight nuns could not possibly be more than a fly's speck in the king's budget. Besides, we have been fending for ourselves through Napoleon's wars. And what about the others, myself included? Where would I go?"

"Back home to your families," the corporal says. "King

Maximilian is prepared to pay a small pension."

Abbess Mayrin claps together her hands, the sound strange and surprisingly loud. "How lucky for me."

I never knew that our Abbess could be sarcastic, and despite this terrible situation, I have to smile.

"Tell your king or whoever you report to that we will discuss the matter and decide on it by the day after tomorrow."

Corporal Maier opens his mouth, then closes it. Without a word, he disappears.

CHAPTER FIFTEEN

All night, I lie awake as the scenes from yesterday repeat themselves in my head. By now, most of Sabiona's most sacred possessions are surely gone. Again, men have taken over the abbey, are moving into the main house, infesting holy ground.

Forget it, your abbey is no more.

But in my heart, it is. Nuns have lived up here for more than a hundred years. I have lived here for a third of that time, thirty-four years, my entire adult existence. For the farmers of Tirol, who toil in the valleys, Sabiona is a holy place, a refuge and destination of pilgrimage. Visitors come here to pray and be close to God.

And now some strange government declares Sabiona nonexistent, without meaning? It is simply a block of stone on a mountaintop?

The fury I have worked so hard to contain rears through me with such force, I throw my blanket off to fan my heated skin. How dare they!

As dawn sends its first gray fingers into my cell, I wash and dress. My mind is made up and nothing and nobody will change it.

Abbess Mayrin has trouble walking this morning, so I help her to a seat in our dining room. It is early and the new occupants are quiet so far.

"I have a suggestion," I say, well aware that our vow of silence during meals has begun. Extraordinary times require extraordinary measures.

The Abbess tilts her head the slightest bit to indicate she is listening.

"I will remain here and—"

"Child, not again, it is too dangerous."

I shake my head. "I will not leave! I remained when the French came. I will stay now. These are just Bavarians, Austria's neighbors."

Abbess Mayrin lowers her gaze.

"I know it is dangerous. But where would I go? I am not going to teach and I will certainly not return home." *What home*, my mind mocks. Exactly!

"They will turn Sabiona into a fortress," Abbess Mayrin says. "The churches are being destroyed…"

"But it is holy ground… for us… for the people of this land."

"Made unholy and soiled by heathens from the north."

I nod. The young novice, Sister Benedikta, is carrying in a tray of breadbaskets. I pour tea for the Abbess and myself, then follow her lead and sink into silence to pray.

God, show me the way, show me what I should do. Last time I stayed, I was a lot younger and stronger.

The words echo through my head as I urge them to rise and meet God's ear. Is he listening or has he completely abandoned us? Is this another trial to test our resolve?

I taste nothing of the bread, chew and swallow mechanically. It is unimportant. Only the abbey counts. Without us, my life, what I have considered my purpose, will lose all meaning. Again, heat rises from my belly up my throat until I tug at the coif to release it. No matter what Benedict preaches, I am angry. Weak too, but mostly angry.

In the end, six of us decide to stay: Gertrud and Dorothea, the young novice, Benedikta, a couple of older nuns, and me. I smile grimly as Abbess Mayrin, surrounded by our sisters, walks toward the tunnels. She moves slowly and leans on a cane, my sisters carry her bag. It will be a difficult journey, but we decided it would be too risky for her to stay. She will seek refuge with one of the farming families in Klausen.

As we wave good-bye—Benedikta and Gertrud are crying silently—a half dozen people, three men and three women, approach with two wooden carts. The men are neither Bavarian soldiers, nor do these women belong into an abbey.

Clearly, the three of them are of an entirely different profession with their colored cheeks, deep necklines and wild hair. I may have been living away from society, but I recognize a prostitute when I see one. Neither of them meets my gaze until they are almost past. Only then does the one with black hair and a brightly painted mouth throw me a nasty glance.

"Sister Magdalena?" A tall figure in a priest's habit enters from the gloom of the tunnel, a mild smile on his lips. "Do you not recognize me?"

I take in the hulking figure, the curved nose. "Herr Haspinger, you arrive at a most difficult time." He has aged and must be in his thirties now.

The smile broadens. "Father Joachim now. I belong to the Capuchin Congregation."

I make a face. "This time, the Bavarian king has declared us obsolete."

Haspinger nods as a crease deepens between his brows. "It is one reason why I am here. We were forced to vacate our monastery in Schlanders. Supposedly, it is our fault that the people are unhappy." He scoffs. "I was relocated to the central cloister in Klausen. It is mayhem down there. I sleep on the floor, we do not have enough cells, not to mention food."

I stare at the young priest who is so well spoken. "It is a shame what they do to this country, to the people… to us."

He looks over his shoulder as if someone is lurking in the bushes. "I am being watched. I guess they dislike what I have to say."

"Please join us, tell us about your travels."

"I cannot stay long."

As we make our way toward the main house, the black-haired woman with the red lips jeers, "What are they still doing here?" The men accompanying her are no better, their clothes ragged and dirty, and their mouths full of rotten teeth. They cackle and whisper to each other about us.

Resentment lies in my mouth like the bitter elixir I make from dandelion root, wormwood and milk thistle for ailments of the intestines. I consider a reply, something sharp and witty. I say nothing, thankful for Father Joachim's calming presence. Surely the Bavarians will send them off.

But no, the Bavarian occupiers just look on as the six ruffians are unloading their wares. The woman with the black hair is catcalling after a couple of young Bavarian soldiers, whose cheeks turn pink as they march past. It does not take much imagination to know what will happen here soon.

I introduce Father Joachim to Gertrud, Benedikta and Dorothea, who have been watching the invasion open-mouthed. Together we lead them away. Gertrud's blue eyes flash in anger, but she follows without comment. She has matured a lot since her arrival, which feels like centuries ago.

"What are they doing here?" she asks as soon as we are out of earshot. "This is neither a county fair nor an inn."

"I am afraid it is not for us to decide," I say. "Let us visit with Father Joachim for a while. He has been here before, remember?"

Once again, we are in the guesthouse, where Gertrud prepares peppermint tea, slices of bread and cucumber. Father Joachim appears happy to sit peacefully.

"I'm in exile. The military showed up in the middle of the night. The officer who escorted us from our monastery overheard me saying 'that maybe soon, we would escort them somewhere.'" Father Joachim sighs. "He denounced me at the local judge and now I am being stalked."

"They know about your brave deeds in the past," I say. And to the others, "Father Joachim was one of the first visitors here in 1796, leading our local fighters."

"Since my ordination three years ago, I have been traveling the country, holding mass, listening to the common folk." He shakes his head. "It is the same no matter where I turn. The people resent foreign rule, they were tired of the French, now they want to see Bavarians leave. One wonders what the leadership of these countries thinks."

"Mostly, they want power."

"And the assets of the church," Father Joachim adds. "Bavaria has seized lands and riches from everyone connected to the church."

"That is why I don't understand what they want with Sabiona," I say. "We barely have enough to make it through the year."

"Apparently, it is the opposite," Gertrud cries. "King Maximilian I is worried, *he* has to support *us*."

I scoff. "No matter the situation, we have always made it through. If nothing else, the villagers help us."

"It is harassment." Father Joachim leans back and folds his hands. "But it will not last. Mark my words, the tide will swing the other way soon. I have spoken with Andreas Hofer numerous times."

Gertrud leans forward, obviously fascinated by our visitor. "Who is he?"

Father Joachim chuckles quietly. "Andreas runs the Sand Inn in the Passeier valley and is a force to be reckoned with. He is a freedom fighter who has been rousing our farmers. I have heard his speeches, met him several times."

"What can one man accomplish?" Benedikta's voice is hardly audible. "I am just so afraid."

Gertrud pats her hand. "Me too."

Father Joachim takes a sip of tea. "It is challenging to see from up here, but I can tell you, Andreas Hofer will make a difference. People like and follow him. Let us trust that God will give him strength and protect him."

"How much longer?" escapes from my lips. "They want all of us to leave again."

"I wish I knew." Father Joachim rises and looks at me. "Remember last time. It will pass, however difficult it may seem. "Now I'd better go, before they pick me up again."

"Be careful… watch yourself… go with God," we all cry.

Father Joachim turns to me. "Sister Magdalena, will you accompany me to the gate?"

I bow my head. "Of course."

"There is one other reason why I wanted to speak with you," he says as soon as we are out of earshot. He hesitates, but then continues, "I think you remember Georg Teiner?"

I throw him a curious glance as a lump of ice spreads through me. "How would you—"

Father Joachim stops abruptly and faces me. "I once saw him with you… a Tirolean soldier pestering a nun. It made me curious."

"You noticed," I whisper.

Father Joachim takes my right hand. "I kept an eye on him, at least while he was under my watch. He told some of the men about you, that you two were engaged."

"I could not—"

"You had your reasons, I am sure." Our eyes meet. "Georg Teiner died a few months ago. He was quite ill for a while, could hardly walk and lost the use of his right hand."

I sigh deeply, think about our last encounter, the bloody bandage. "I think he was sick for a long time."

Father Joachim nods. "I thought you should know."

"Thank you."

After the priest disappears into the tunnel, I remain staring after him. Georg is dead. I am surprised to feel a vague sadness, a melancholy. He was a difficult and cruel man, maybe his last years gave him time to reflect. I turn my face upward and say a quick prayer. If anyone knows how to handle Georg, it is God.

Back at the guesthouse, I address my sisters. "Let us visit the church for a while."

Wordlessly, the others follow me, a few bedraggled and sad nuns who have lost their world—again. Only Gertrud throws me a curious glance.

"What was that all about?" she asks as she catches up

to me.

"He wants me to take care of you all." Inwardly, I shudder. Lying is a sin, but I cannot share my secret, not even with Gertrud, who nods thoughtfully. She knows it is a lie.

Thankfully there is a distraction, though not the kind I would wish for. The doors of the Church of the Holy Cross gape wide open. Bavarian soldiers are removing benches, altar and sculptures.

"What is the meaning of this?" I cry at the next man who walks past with a small Jesus statue under his arm. "You are stealing our things."

The man just shrugs and resumes his walk. The next two leaving the church are carrying a side table with inlaid wood between them. "It is best you go," one of them says, an ugly grin on his face. "Haven't you heard that the abbey is closed?"

"Have you no conscience?" I shout. "This is not yours to take, it is the property of the church."

"What church?" the man mocks.

"You'd better leave before somebody gets hurt," a voice says from behind. I turn just as Corporal Maier abruptly stops in front of me. "If you make trouble, I will order your removal."

"No trouble, Corporal," I say, hoping my eyes are as steely as those of a man. "Just wondering why you allow this criminal behavior. Even if your kind ordered the closure of our abbey, does it mean you should steal? Not even the French did that."

"I simply follow General Fenner's orders."

"Maybe I should speak to him."

The corporal chuckles as if I made a delightful joke. "For one, he is in Bolzano. Secondly, he has no time for the likes of you. Time to go, Sister." Maier may not be tall, but he could throw me down with a swipe of his hand.

"Come." Gertrud sends the other nuns back to the guesthouse, takes my elbow and leads me down the path.

I lower my head to hide my tears, and only when we

arrive in the main house do I allow them to flow. Footsteps echo in the halls as we huddle in the former office of Abbess Mayrin that has been stripped of all things personal or valuable. Where the little Jesus above the desk used to hang, a figure I have often looked to when approaching difficult subjects with Abbess Mayrin, King Maximilian's likeness stares.

I recognize the voice of the black-haired woman, her common laugh. She is making herself comfortable within our holy walls. Father Joachim's voice echoes through my head: it will pass. *When*, I want to shout, *when will we ever be left in peace?*

"Let us return to the guesthouse." The words take so much effort, I can hardly force them out. "This place is neither safe nor becoming."

CHAPTER SIXTEEN

But the guesthouse offers no reprieve. Just the opposite. All
the heartache from ten years ago returns, our suffering at the
hands of the French army, my near escape from an execution.

What is happening now is infinitely worse. The vestige
of our existence is being destroyed as we speak.

"Maybe we should leave as well," Benedikta says. Her
voice is hardly above a whisper, yet easy to hear in the silence
of our despair.

I cannot answer for fear of breaking into a crying fit. I
must do something, anything, but what?

Our meal is silent and we retire to our cells earlier than
usual. My mind feels like an empty vessel. Thoughts tumble in
endless tortuous confusion. In the face of such destruction,
praying seems useless. The corporal will not help, the Abbess
is gone. It is up to us… me… to do something.

We cannot stop the thievery. Nobody can.

But I must try something. Father Joachim spoke about
Andreas Hofer, a single man doing important things. Just one
man. Why not one woman? A nun?

My cell, the same one I lived in when the French
occupied Sabiona, is silent. It is not the calming silence I so
crave, but a cold distant one that frightens and leaves me
uneasy. I sense the despair of my fellow sisters through the

walls, imagine them crying.

At last I rise. It is the hour before dawn and a plan has finally come to me. It is dangerous and mad at the same time, but the time for hesitation is over. *Please, dear Lord, tell me if I should stop. Give me a sign.*

My cell remains silent. Either God has forsaken us or he is punishing me for my sins. New sins of lying and hatred. Old sins from many years ago. Actions I can escape from no easier than my memories and all the prayers in the world will never erase them.

I am back at my father's inn, read the anger in his expression. "I will not marry Georg," I say, knowing it will incense him further. "I cannot." Mother sits at the table, crying silent tears. She has never spoken up to Father, she will not help me now.

"It is arranged," my father says. "Now go and serve our guests."

I run from the kitchen, half blind with rage. All evening, I fetch beer, deliver platters of meat and dumplings. I hear none of the crude jokes or friendly banter of our guests, my movements mechanical and my mind far away.

Georg, the man I am supposed to marry, is a farmer from a neighboring valley, a widower, his first wife hardly cold in her grave. Father said that in these times, a man needs a woman by his side, especially when he has small children to tend. The widower is rich and has promised a large sum to my father.

I only encountered him in the inn and my stomach turns just imagining him near. It is not so much his body that turns my innards, but the ice in his eyes. It is a coldness of the soul, a lack of mercy I have not seen in other men. No wonder his first wife left him. Rumor has it she hanged herself in the barn. I know I will not hear the truth from my father or this man.

"Sister Magdalena?" Gertrud's voice, paired with a soft knock, brings me back.

"Come in, I am up," I say.

In the shine of the single candle, I see that Gertrud has been crying. She throws herself into my arms and begins anew. Great big sobs fill the room and I let her tears wet my tunic.

"May… be we need to go," she finally says. "I cannot bear watching them."

I rub Gertrud's back, then hold her at arm's length. "I am going to leave for a few days. Promise me to stay until the end of the week."

Gertrud wipes her face. "Where will you go?"

I shake my head. "It is best if you do not know, in case this corporal notices my absence."

"But—"

I place a forefinger on Gertrud's lips. "Trust me."

Gertrud's eyes have always been like mirrors of her soul and right now they reflect confusion, sadness but also hope.

Recognizing how my words have added to this hope, my resolve is firm. I must do what I planned, no matter how crazy or dangerous it is. But first…

"What will I tell the others?" Gertrud asks.

"That I went to secure provisions."

Gertrud looks doubtful but says nothing.

"There is one thing I need your help with," I say reluctantly. "Remember that time when you pretended to twist your ankle?"

"To distract the French soldier?"

"Yes." I cannot help but smile, remembering Gertrud's cries and the French man's attentions. "I will need you to divert one more time."

Gertrud's eyes grow large. "What will you do?"

But I only shake my head. "Be ready when I tell you."

After six o'clock prayers of *Prime* in the kitchen, I send Benedikta and Dorothea to the gardens. The two older nuns will prepare our quarters, stock up firewood and prepare our meals. A cool mist blankets the mountain this morning as Gertrud and I hurry toward the main house.

Yesterday, I noticed that the Bavarians have repurposed our library as a storage room. Men carried assorted items inside and I am hoping to find what I need there.

Except for a few echoing snores, the halls are deserted. Already, the formerly spotless floors are soiled with mud and spit.

"I need something from the library," I whisper before we turn the corner to the main hallway.

"But we cleared it," Gertrud says.

"They are using it now."

"You are going to steal?" Surprise rings in Gertrud's voice.

"Why not?" The words are out before I can stop them. "Actually, I will borrow something." I am distracted because my gaze has fallen on a trunk piled high with clothes. When I look at Gertrud, she watches me curiously. "I need you to leave now. Just tell them I am looking to secure supplies."

"I want to come with you."

I take Gertrud's hand in mine. "You are one of my truest sisters, my friend, but it is too dangerous. Just pray for me." I look to the door and listen, ignore Gertrud's pleading eyes. "Now go."

As soon as Gertrud has left, I sort through the stack, pick what I need, and hide the bundle under my robe.

As I sneak toward the exit, I notice the woman with the black hair and deep neckline carrying one of our crosses over her shoulder. I want to rip it from her dirty hands. Instead, I hurry on. What I must do is more important.

Near the gate stand two Bavarian soldiers. I nod at them and march wordlessly into the morning.

CHAPTER SEVENTEEN

The village of Klausen is barely awake as I pass the narrow streets, cross the bridge and ascend the next hill. It is a steep trail, rocks slide beneath my feet. When I pass a shelter used by traveling merchants, I stop. It is a rough-hewn cabin not unlike the one I stopped at so many years ago. Inside, it smells of wood dust and soot.

I slide out the package I have been carrying from under my habit, take off my coif and veil. I look at the items, the stained beige pants and leggings, the vest, coat and epaulets, the black hat. Everything reeks of sweat and worse. With a wrinkled nose, I slide the tunic over my head. There is no turning back. Not now. Too much is at stake.

I put everything on, twist up my hair and stick it under the hat. For once, I wish for a looking glass. I feel exposed, almost naked. I am used to hiding most of my face, my entire body, really. Now I am dressed like a man. Not just any man, but a soldier of the French army. Our enemy.

Carefully, lovingly, I fold up my habit, coif and veil, pack everything in the shoulder bag I carry along.

All day I hike, taking short breaks to catch my breath or drinking a bit of water from the many mountain creeks. The piece of bread in my pack is calling to me, but I must be strong. I have got to climb a lot longer. In the afternoon, I cross over the Villanderer Mountain toward the Rittner, a massive mountain to the south.

My body feels heavy, each step requires all my will. The trail is so steep, I have to lean forward not to lose my balance. Small rocks make the path slippery, and I am thankful for my winter boots, even if they do not fit with the rest of my disguise.

The sun has set and dusk settles. With it, temperatures drop. My breath steams, though I am not cold, just so bone tired. With my hair under the hat, the skin on my neck is exposed and icy. Doubt creeps up in me. Maybe from a distance, I pass as a soldier—some skinny man who is surprisingly clean shaven. But close up, I will be found out instantly.

As darkness settles over the mountains, my thoughts wander back to the time when I was on the run. I was so young back then, did not know what to do. I had thought I had killed the man I was supposed to marry.

He may have been my betrothed, but he was cruel like my father. No, worse! A sound escapes me, a howl like a wounded animal. I never allow myself to think about the night when Georg lured me from the taproom. He had been drinking all evening, encouraged by my father, who could not wait to get his hands on Georg's wedding gift, a wooden chest filled with silver thaler.

Georg had told me to come upstairs, he had a surprise. Why had I not seen through it? Why not insisted he should give it to me in the tavern room?

Indeed, he had had a gift for me. Some gold trinket that broke in the ensuing struggle. He had pulled me to him, towered over me, a man muscled from daily work and many pounds heavier. He reeked of alcohol and sweat, his grip around my wrists like iron cuffs. I had tried to fend him off, my fists pushed uselessly against his massive chest.

"You will be my wife soon enough, so quit your crying."

"Please," was all I could get out.

He laughed roughly and pushed me against the wall, tugged at my skirt. All the while, his stinking breath was upon me, his lips wet with spittle as his tongue sought entry into my mouth. I wiggled and shook, but his weight alone was too much.

He managed to pull up my skirt and to this day, I feel his rough hand touch me. And then…

I let out another howl. The air is so cold, it hurts to breathe.

The pain of Georg's attack never left, the filth he introduced, the feeling of utter helplessness. I had had only a rough idea what a man and a woman did after marriage, but was utterly unprepared for such an assault. He pushed against me, grunted like a man possessed.

My right arm fell away to the side, just as he finished and bent low to close his trousers. My fingers closed around the brass candle holder. I smacked it over his skull in a hard sweep. Much harder than I had thought possible. Blood spurted and as he sagged to the ground, I scrambled over him and forced my aching body to the door.

To this day, I remember standing in the hallway, listening to my father talking loudly to his guests. I still feel the panic.

My breath ragged, I gripped my throat and let go immediately because it was tender from Georg's grip. What was I to do? Inside that room lay my betrothed, who I had murdered. No matter what he had done to me, a man was worth so much more than his lowly fiancée. They would put me away, maybe sentence me to death. I could not stay. Any moment my father would call for me, any moment someone would search for Georg.

Without making a sound, I tiptoed to the stairs, down each step, slipped through the corridor to the backdoor, outside. It was cold, so cold, and every bit of me wanted to return to the warmth of my home. However faulty, it was the place I knew with a bed and a fire in the hearth.

Again, I am outside, climbing mountain paths, only this

time I know where I am going. I have no choice, this is the last effort, my last chance.

Somewhere I stop and rest on a boulder. Above, millions of stars sparkle like ice crystals. The immensity of it makes me feel small, unimportant. I chew the bread, slowly and deliberately. It has to sustain me a bit longer.

The last hour before dawn, I can hardly move my legs. In front of me lies the valley of Bolzano, a long, beautiful basin. Even up here, I feel the temperature rising with each descending step until I sweat in my unaccustomed outfit. How am I ever going to make it through town in broad daylight? Everyone will see through me. They will laugh and lock me away.

A clump of soldiers walks my way, loudly talking. Afraid of them, I slip into the parish church of the Assumption of Mary.

In the semi-dark, I breathe deeply. As usual, the incense gives me a bit of assurance. Behind the high altar, I find the image of holy Mary and throw myself at her feet; they say she has special powers. Nobody knows where the image came from, but the story is that a wagoner was traveling through the moss, which is how the area was called in those days, and heard a fine voice. He saw nobody and wanted to continue when the voice spoke again, "Pick me up." The wagoner stopped his carriage and discovered Mary's shimmering image on the ground. He picked it up and decided to honor her with a small chapel right at this spot. Many years later, the chapel was enlarged into a church, this church, and the image is still here.

Please, holy mother of God, give me strength and bravery to fulfill my task. I lie there on that cold stone and pray like I never have before. The strange thing is, I do not feel cold. A warm swirling energy makes me rise and bow my head to Mary.

Then I march outside.

CHAPTER EIGHTEEN

The streets are filling with people as I rush past. I was here many years ago, when Father looked for new suppliers, have come here with Mother to shop for linens. The town has changed dramatically. Men in French and Bavarian uniforms march past, horse-drawn carriages and wagons throw up dust.

Twice I stop to get my bearings. I am afraid to ask for directions, but at last I recognize the commandant's house, a two-story structure with large windows shaded by palm trees. At the entry, two soldiers stand guard.

Pulling myself up to appear as tall as possible, I say in a strong voice, "I must speak to General Fenner."

If the guard thinks I look strange, he doesn't let on. He keeps his eyes on my face and says, "You have an appointment, I am sure."

"No, sir, but it is of utmost urgency."

The man appears to struggle with my answer, but after a minute or so, he nods and disappears while the other guard places himself in the middle of the doorway, as if I would charge through.

Several more minutes pass. Heat rises from inside my coat. I am unfamiliar with the balmy air of this area and have the urge to take it off. My throat is dry, my teeth feel gritty and my throat burns with thirst, but I cannot let that stop me.

Thirty-six years of self-denial have formed me. I have to turn my attention away from my ailing body, Mary is at my side.

"Come!" The guard waves at me to follow him. "Make it quick, the general is a busy man."

"Yes, sir."

General Fenner sits behind an ornate desk that is covered in maps of all sizes.

"Sir... General, thank you for seeing me."

Fenner remains seated and hardly looks up. "You are?"

"Sister Magdalena from Sabiona Abbey."

General Fenner's head shoots up, curiosity plays on his face, a bit of amusement, maybe. "It is a curious disguise, Sister. What brings you all this way?"

This is it, this is the moment I have gone over in my mind a thousand times. I want to speak forcefully, release my anger, but instead my knees buckle. I fall to the ground and look up at the powerful man.

"I beg you, sir, Sabiona has been defiled. Our books and parchments, our holy vessels, even our furniture has been stolen, sold to the highest bidder. Common folk, women are moving in to service the soldiers—the abbey is becoming a cesspool. Sabiona has been there for so many years, it is a holy place, a sanctuary for the people. Pilgrims come to find peace within its walls."

I struggle for air, force another breath through my tightening throat. I cannot cry now. "Sir, it is a cruelty we cannot bear. Surely God is looking down to test us. I have come to see you, I—"

"You have come all this way?"

"I walked," I say. I am still on the ground, Fenner can simply sweep me from the room. "Across the Villanderer Mountain and the Rittner."

"Why so far? Isn't there a much easier route through the valley?"

I let out a sigh and look at the man behind his desk. "There is, sir, but I could not risk being stopped by your men. Any men, for that matter."

"Sister Magdalena, I must say." Fenner straightens and walks around the desk. He holds out an arm. Again, I marvel at my luck. I do not think I could get up by myself right then. My knees are stiff and my lower back demands rest. "Please take a seat." Fenner guides me to a chair. "You disguised yourself as a soldier to gain entry here?" Returning to his seat, he shakes his head. Is that a smirk on his face?

"Sir, I—"

Fenner raises an arm to cut me off. "If I understand you correctly, soldiers and intruders have stripped the abbey of its valuables."

I nod. "Surely there must be something you can do. Surely there are other more suitable places for these soldiers to set up camp."

Fenner looks thoughtful. He bends over his maps, mumbles something and finally looks up.

"Sister Magdalena, the fact you took this journey yourself shows me how much you love Sabiona." He nods more to himself. "I will think it over." Our eyes meet. "These are busy, uncertain times, you understand. I cannot promise…"

I raise my hands as if I want to pray. "I thank you for whatever you can do."

He points to the door. I am dismissed.

As I rise, the room begins to spin. I must show strength, but I have not eaten more than a bit of bread and my body refuses to obey me any longer. The last thing I see is the ornate tile floor rushing up to me.

"Sister?" The general's face appears above me. I must have fainted because all of a sudden, three or four men surround me.

"Fetch the doctor," is the last thing I hear. When I come to again, I am lying on a cot in a darkened room. A man with a bald head whose face and nose speak of too much wine is bending over me.

"Sister?" he says, obviously relieved I am waking up.

I scramble to sit, not wanting a man so close to me.

Immediately, the room begins spinning and I lie back.

The man clears his throat. "I should examine you."

"Thank you," I huff. "All I need is some food and water."

With a nod, he straightens and hurries from the room, obviously glad he can skip examining a nun in men's attire.

This time, I sit up slowly. The walls settle, I can focus again. Across from me, a full-length mirror shows a strange figure in a soldier's uniform.

Is it really me? In Sabiona, there are no mirrors. Sisters are not supposed to be vain and have no need to look at themselves. But this person… this strange appearance. I step closer, see the figure approach. Her eyes are still dark, only her hair shows gray streaks, a side of her she has kept hidden for more than thirty years. Her face shows lines she does not recognize.

When have I last looked at myself? I think back to the pub, my room above, the alcohol vapors, the smoke from dozens of pipes… voices rising as the hours grew late.

I had considered myself safe up there, until Georg destroyed it all. He and my father Anton, who had schemed together. Had encouraged Georg to court me. But Georg was not a man to be content with a few conversations, a few walks through the village. He had wanted more, he had wanted all of me.

A sigh escapes me. Will the pain ever fade?

The sounds of men shouting commands and marching feet trickle through the window. My discomfort returns. Frankly, I am embarrassed. Even when the French occupied Sabiona, I never showed such weakness. I have to leave quickly, but as soon as I stand up, the ache in my middle increases and my vision blurs.

Please, holy mother of God, let me get out of here in one piece. But in my state, I am unsure I can leave town, much less hike many hours.

I sit there, praying to Mary, when the door opens once more. A young soldier sets a tray at the corner of my cot, nods and slips away without a word.

What does it matter? An incredible aroma reaches my nose. The tray holds a bowl of stew, bread, an apple, a glass of red wine and a carafe of water.

I smile.

CHAPTER NINETEEN

I do not remember how long it takes me to get to my next stop. I am traveling the valley paths this time, do not have the strength. Nor do I want to spend additional time away from the abbey.

The bishop's residence is located north in Brixen, past Klausen village. Thankfully, Bishop Karl Franz von Lodron welcomes me without showing the slightest bit of surprise, though it must be after nine o'clock at night. He surely hears a lot of stories during confession, though I am sure he has never seen a nun dressed in a French soldier's garment. Only when I tell him about my visit with General Fenner do his eyes grow large.

"You are a brave soul, Sister Magdalena. I will do what I can." He folds his hands and looks at me thoughtfully. "Now I urge you to rest."

Though the Bishop lost all his land through secularization five years ago, he is rumored to be a generous man, sharing what is left with the needy.

My legs burn as I climb uphill to Sabiona. It is dark and every step sends darts of pain up my spine. The muscles in my legs threaten to seize up any moment. Why have I declined the bishop's offer to spend the night? Was it pride? At least my stomach is calm from a generous meal the bishop provided.

But I am paying the price for my stubbornness. Four times I rest, but as soon as I straighten, the agony returns. My steps slow to a crawl. I try to draw air, a freezing early-morning air that sends chills through me. Even in summer, the mountains can be cold, the air chilly. I have always loved Sabiona for its crisp clean air, which has undoubtedly fouled under the Bavarian occupation.

As the first light of dawn creeps across the mountain, the walls of Sabiona rise in front of me. In the past, its sight has always brought gladness to my heart. Now all I feel is heaviness and a dread of what I will find inside.

"Stop right there!" a voice calls from the gate.

Only now do I remember that I have not changed back into my habit.

"I am Sister Magdalena," I say to the looming figure.

Two guards, one with a lantern, the other with a gun, approach. "You are who?" The man swings his light in front of my face, then steps back a couple of feet to take in my outfit. "Would you look at that?" he laughs. "What a jester! A woman dressed as a man, pretending to be a nun?"

His friend laughs even louder. "I have never seen or heard anything like it. Surely she is lying."

I scold myself for having been so careless and not discarded the uniform. Again, I feel naked, exposed, my face and neck without coif and veil, the shape of my body clearly visible in the dreaded men's uniform. "Here is my habit." I hold up the bag I have carried all this way. "It was a ruse to travel more safely."

"Really, where did you go?" the man with the lantern asks.

"I did not think nuns traveled much," says his companion.

None of your business, I want to say. Instead, I force my mouth into a mild smile. "I wanted to find more provisions for our abbey. So we can all eat."

The man with the lantern spits. "It is no more an abbey

than my shoe. And you might as well throw away that stupid tunic. We do not need all that religious nonsense anymore."

I am no longer cold, want to rip at the scratchy collar, because the fury in me boils at the man's words. But decades of self-control come in handy. Besides, I do not have the strength. Again, I smile mildly. "Be that as it may, I would like to join my sisters in the guesthouse. Surely you do not mind me helping to secure provisions."

The two guards look at each other, and finally wave me through. "I would take that sham off, sister. Before you get shot," one of them calls after me.

The abbey has suffered even more in my absence. Rubbish litters our gardens and paths, a horrible stench clings to everything. What if General Fenner does not follow through? It was bad enough when the French were here, King Maximilian's army is worse. Now the abbey has lost its innards and its identity.

I breathe a sigh of relief when I enter the guesthouse. I am so tired, the air in front of me appears to flicker. Please, God, let me get to my room.

"Magda!" Sister Gertrud, who has been baking bread, flies to my side. "What happened, where have you been? I was so worried. You never said how long…" She steps back and stares at me. "You look terrible. And you are wearing men's clothes?"

I hear the disgust in her voice, but still have to grin. "I'd better change right away before the others see me. Will you be so kind as to fetch me water to wash?"

I can tell how urgently Gertrud wants to question me, but to her credit, she rushes to the stove to pick up a pot of hot water. "Quick, quick, before the sisters return from prayer."

In my room, Gertrud pours water into the bowl, mixes it with cold, lays out soap, towel and wash cloth and hurries to the door. "I shall fix you a bit of bread. You look all pinched."

With a sigh, I peel out of the soldier's outfit, wash from top to bottom and return to my beloved habit. Then I sag onto the bed and pass out.

When I awake, dusk is settling. Next to me sits a cup of peppermint tea, a plate with bread, a boiled egg and steamed apples. I eat quietly, feel the nourishment strengthen my body.

The sisters hover in the kitchen and have obviously waited for me, because as soon as I enter, they all jump up and surround me, the room fills with excited chatter. I do not think I have ever heard so much talk at the same time.

Gertrud runs to me, takes my hands in hers. "What did you do? I prayed for your safety."

I lower my head. "I am sorry to have worried you. It was easier and safer for everyone to keep it to myself."

Our eyes meet, Gertrud's are full of tears. The others crowd around me, touch my arms as if they want to make sure that I am really here. They all talk at once. "Where have you been? We missed you so!"

"Let her speak." Gertrud leads me to a seat as if I were an invalid.

Again, dread rises in me. If I tell of my travels and the general and Bishop von Lodron do not succeed, I will just cause my sisters more disappointment.

"How have you fared?" I ask instead, looking around the room. I know that this is not what they want to hear.

Only Gertrud humors me. "It is tolerable, just barely, as long as we stay here. They even removed the church pews. Some were burned, others carried off."

I feel the despair in the room as surely as I feel my own. Even if they remain silent, they all wonder what will happen to us. Our home, our purpose has been stripped away, stolen by ruffians and ruthless men—again.

"Will you not tell us about your travels?" Dorothea studies me carefully. A bit of stubbornness has returned from the old days.

I consider making up a visit with the Abbess. But I have sinned enough for a lifetime, I will not lie to the people who are my family. "Please forgive me, I will tell you all later."

I close my mouth, look at each of my sisters. "I am just so thankful to be back here… with you."

"Maybe we should pray?" Benedikta offers.

We all lower our heads. Prayer is typically an enlightening affair, an exchange with God that leaves me feeling better and sometimes a bit wiser. Not today. Today, the room's air is thick with heavy thoughts, the fear and doubts of half a dozen nuns. We are not equipped to deal with the politics of men, their ways, the constant warring.

Please God, holy Mother Mary, anyone who will hear me, send help. Let the goodness in humankind prevail, let them see the light.

A noise travels through the thick walls. Somewhere voices shout, feet, many feet hurry through the gardens.

I whisper an amen and slowly rise. Next to me the nuns stir, some wipe tears from their cheeks.

Without a second thought, I march to the door.

"Magda," cries Gertrud. "This time, I will not let you walk alone."

I pat her arm. "I just need to see what is going on."

"We will all go." Dorothea and Benedikta are clasping hands together, so are the older two sisters.

Inside me, I pray for patience. I would much rather go alone. "It may be dangerous," I say, hurrying to the door. "What if there is another attack?"

But my fellow sisters ignore me. They obviously have little patience left themselves.

Slowly, like a procession, we move toward the main house, where men in Austrian uniform rush this way and that. Some are on horseback, others on foot, all carry guns.

A woman cries out and shouts profanities. It is the one with the black hair. She pumps her fist at the men, who ignore her outburst. As she passes by us, our eyes meet.

"Damn nuns," she cries.

I remain silent, just nod at her while hope rises inside me like a hymn. *Is it really happening? Is this General Fenner's work?*

More women and men in street clothes are hurrying toward the gate. They carry packs, anger in their expressions.

Other men spill from the entrance to the main house, some curse, some gesticulate. All have one thing in common, they are marching toward the gate.

The Austrian soldiers on horseback tower above, shout orders as more and more people are flushed from the innards of our abbey. Like a thick stream, they are escorted out of Sabiona.

All I feel is glee. I should not, but isn't it a sin, what those people did?

A man in uniform appears in front of us. "I am looking for Sister Magdalena?"

I raise my arm.

"Please follow me, General Fenner would like a word."

I feel the eyes of my fellow sisters on me, but all I say is, "I will explain." And to Gertrud, "Please take the sisters back to our house. We should stay out of their way."

Gertrud's expression shows mutiny. But again, she lowers her head. Gertrud has changed a lot since her earlier days. I cannot help but smile. "I will tell you very soon," I whisper.

General Fenner sits in Abbess Mayrin's former office. As we enter, he is shouting orders to a dozen men, who immediately rush past us. He is red in the face, sweat beads show on his temples.

"Ah, yes, I am sorry." He points at a lone chair in the corner. That is when I discover Abbess Mayrin sitting in a corner chair. She looks at me inquiringly, and even in the gloom, I can tell that she has aged further.

"Mother," is all I can whisper. I had mentioned to Fenner that Abbess Mayrin was in the village.

"Ah, yes. I thought the Abbess would be better off up here." Fenner throws me a quick smile, but turns serious again. "It is as you said. I am afraid there is much to improve. I do not think I can spare any men to help."

"Sir, General?" Abbess Mayrin may be old, but there is still strength in her voice. "What is going on here? Will you make it worse than it already is?"

"Mother, I—"

Fenner raises an arm to cut me off. "I am here to clear Sabiona of its vermin." He throws me a glance, but then looks at Abbess Mayrin. "It appears… Your sister, Magdalena, asked me for help."

This time, I feel the Abbess's eyes boring into my right temple. A knot grows in my throat. "I am sorry, General," I croak. "I did not want to worry the Abbess or my other sisters. They do not know."

The right corner of the general's mouth twitches. Is he smiling again? "Give us a few hours, then all of us shall be gone." He presses his lips together. "I could ask a few of the village people to come and help."

"What about our things?" Abbess Mayrin asks.

"My men are making inquiries and we will send back what we find. I have asked Andreas Hofer to assist us and search for Sabiona's monastic estates."

"Thank you, General," I blurt. How can I express my thankfulness in simple words? I want to hug the man, sing something or at least shake his hand. "I will pray for your continued success," I say instead.

"Sister Magdalena?" Abbess Mayrin's voice is firm. "Will you assist me back to our house? I am sure the general has much to do."

Indeed, Fenner straightens and marches to the door. "I trust you know the way." Then he is gone.

Abbess Mayrin pushes hard on her cane, grunts a bit and faces me. "You still manage to surprise me, Magdalena."

I lower my head. I know I should have told her about my plan. But there was little time to send notes and I know she would have wanted to stop me. In hindsight, it seems folly and full of danger. How could I deceive the one woman who helped me hide my shame?

"I am sorry."

By evening, quiet settles over Sabiona. The gate is closed and not a single commoner or loose woman remains. Gertrud and

I are walking the grounds, inspecting the main quarters. Around every corner, my heart sinks. The filth and destruction are hard to measure, hard to describe. Every room has been defiled, the walls dirty or drawn on, the floors scratched and dirty. The bedding is so filthy, it is gray or brown or… well, it is simply disgusting. I want to burn it all, yet I know we must be frugal and save what we can.

Next to me, Gertrud sighs and sighs again. She is still young, but even she feels disheartened.

"Let us make a list," I say. "Then we will prioritize and see what needs to be done first. Two of us will take a room and address one after the other. I will work on the kitchen." In the back of my mind, I see the little patch of soil I have kept clear of weeds and planted with lavender and a single red rose bush. The lavender has been trampled, the roses pulled out. Something tugs at my heart, a sharp stitch that takes away my breath.

"I will help you." Gertrud's words pull me from my thoughts. She takes my hands, squeezes them hard. "You did this, you went to see the general and saved us… our Sabiona." Tears spill from her eyes, still blue and clear as a mountain lake. "I always knew you were strong, I just never…" She throws her arms up and hugs me.

So, we stand, two nuns, lifelong sisters in good and in bad times. My heart is full.

CHAPTER TWENTY

Spring 1809

Gertrud is shaking her head. "How did you convince Bishop Lodron to reinstate our abbey?" We are sitting outside in a rare moment of reprieve. It is early April, the sky is as clear as the air, a bit frosty, though I do not mind. Since last August, we have cleaned and scraped every inch of the abbey—again. Our sisters have returned and some of the villagers visited for weeks to help. "I still cannot believe you did that. Wore men's clothes and hiked two mountains."

I smile quietly. The skin on my hands feels raw from all the scrubbing. I have also been busy in the gardens, working the soil, planting winter crops. "It had to be done, at least tried."

"You are so brave, Magda."

I had nothing to lose, I want to say. "You are brave as well. You stayed by my side, did not want to return home when the French took over and the Bavarians."

Gertrud scoffs. "Sabiona is the only home I have."

"Mine as well."

We look at each other. I know I should tell her about Georg, about what happened. But Gertrud doesn't seem to notice, her eyes glitter.

"My mother died in childbirth," she says. "Father was

angry… at her, at everyone." Her gaze returns to me. "I was the oldest, took care of my three siblings, the baby." Gertrud's shoulders sag, then her head. "At some point, he thought I should be his wife."

She cries out the last two words, "His wife."

I kneel at Gertrud's side, squeeze her hand. "Oh no, you poor child."

"I was barely seventeen, in love with a boy." A sob rises between us. "Father destroyed it all." She looks at me, her glorious eyes wet now. "I ran away, at first I tried to survive on my own. But everyone wanted… things. Until I heard of the abbey. Mother Mayrin saved me."

"Mother saved me too." It is out before I have time to think.

Gertrud wipes her face, tries a weak smile. "I expected something like it."

"I was to be married to a bad man, my father wanted to force me. So I ran." *Coward. Why do not you tell Gertrud the whole story?* I read in Gertrud's expression that she knows there is more.

Out of the corner of my eye, I notice Benedikta, who is waving frantically. "Come quick, Mother fell."

I have been worrying about Abbess Mayrin ever since she returned. She appears frail these days, almost translucent. She only walks with the help of two sisters and her appetite is waning.

Gertrud and I rush after her to Abbess Mayrin's room. In the gloominess, Sister Juliana sits by Mother's side, a bible in her hand. Juliana, who is also new and used to live in another Austrian convent, is ten years older than me and takes care of the abbey's returned items. She is particularly fond of the archives and has sorted everything anew. For the time being, we keep all our books and historical documents in the guest house.

Mother lies on her bed, but when she hears my steps, her eyes open. She nods at me ever so slightly.

"Will you leave us, please," she says. Juliana and

Gertrud disappear.

"Come here, child."

I kneel next to her, a woman who may as well have been my mother. In fact, she was more of a mother to me than the one who gave birth to me years ago.

"I have asked Juliana to take over as directress. She is now the oldest and even though she is new here, she has much administrative experience." She pats my hand. "I did not think you would be interested."

She is right. I am not. Besides, my latest adventure has likely been proof in the Abbess's eyes that I am not material to lead our nuns. And there is the other thing.

"We will have a celebration tomorrow." Abbess Mayrin chuckles. "If I make it that long."

"Of course, you will." I kiss her hand. "I am glad you do not have to work so hard anymore."

Again, that chuckle. "Magda, you and I know that my days are quite numbered. I am ready to meet God, I am at peace." She searches for my eyes. "Are you at peace, my child?"

Momentarily, I am speechless. What is she talking about?

Her eyes, which have lost most of their color and are watery gray, are serious. "Have you forgiven yourself? I am sure God has."

My mouth opens and closes as Mother's features blur. My throat is clogged and does not allow me to speak.

"You did nothing wrong, child." Mother's feeble hand grips mine. Her skin feels papery thin. "Those men, your father and…"

"Georg?"

"Yes, Georg. They put you through hell and still, ever since, you have been working so hard, taking many risks."

In my mind, I am back in Abbess Mayrin's room. I see the blood, so much blood puddling between my legs. I see her leading me to her bed and helping me deliver my baby. Much too early, it is tiny and yet perfect. Created from a terrible sin.

The image of Mother wrapping her into a blanket is the

last thing I remember before I fell asleep.

I realize I have wanted to justify my life up here at the abbey. Have done all I can to preserve my home. Because I have no other. Not since that night many years ago, when Georg forced himself on me.

A sob escapes me, then another.

Abbess Mayrin's fingertips touch the back of my hand. "You have done nothing to be ashamed of. It is no sin to mourn the loss of your child."

"You never told me, you never…"

Twice I had asked Mother about the baby. Once right after birth, when I awoke and my baby was gone. But Abbess Mayrin never answered, not then, not three years later, when I asked a second time. She had simply shaken her head.

My baby's death bound me to Sabiona more tightly than a thousand ropes and I told myself I would see her after my death, that we would reunite.

"You saved the abbey, Mariele. You alone saved her. I always knew God had larger plans for you." Now Mother's eyes are filled with tears. "Your heart is large. I pray that history will never forget your deeds. So many of us and all those villagers and pilgrims will thank you forever."

I squeeze Abbess Mayrin's hand because I still cannot talk. But obviously, she is not done yet. "Let Juliana take over now. You enjoy some time in the garden and kitchen, pray and work with the other sisters… like you were meant to all these years."

"Thank you," I croak. "For all you have done. For being a mother to me." I want to say so much more, but words, oh complicated wondrous words, you fail me. I have kept things locked up for so long, they are stuck inside me.

The Abbess just looks at me with such love, I burst into tears. "Your baby is safe." She sighs deeply and closes her eyes.

I snap to. "What do you mean?"

Mother's eyes open once more. "She was small, but she is alive."

"But I thought… I thought—"

"I know." The Abbess's eyes are closed again. "I am sorry." After a while, her breathing is even. Abbess Mayrin, keeper of Sabiona and my secret, is sleeping.

I stare at the old woman as the words "safe" and "alive" swirl through my head. Some place out there, my girl lives.

I tiptoe outside and find my room to hide.

CHAPTER TWENTY-ONE

April/May 1809

Father Joachim sits in the courtyard and fans himself, a few of us nuns gathered around him. The sun barely breaks through the clouds today and the wind remains cool, but the priest is red in the face and fans himself. He has obviously rushed here to see us.

"The Tirolean revolution is in full swing," he says. "It started on April 9, when the Bavarian king was trying to forcibly recruit Tirolean men. Ha, he should not have done that. Andreas Hofer gathered his sharpshooters and has been fighting Bavarian and French armies ever since. Innsbruck capitulated and the Bavarians have left." He takes a deep breath. "Though it has been bloody at times."

"Will you stay a while to rest?" I ask, while my thoughts wander to the girl I once bore and who is out there some place, maybe in harm's way, maybe sick or injured. What is her life like, what is she thinking about this crazy war that finds no end? I push away the thought and concentrate on our visitor.

Father Joachim runs a hand through his generous beard that reaches to his chest and seems to be aflame. "No time. I have been made captain of a commando of sharpshooters. The enemy is everywhere. I have asked Salzburg to join us." He chuckles. "They call me Father

Redbeard."

"How many men?"

"Hofer commands eighteen thousand."

I try to imagine the magnitude of so many Tiroleans encountering an equal number of Bavarians and French, especially in the mountains. Impossible. I feel crowded with a few dozen people.

"Maybe you will pray for us? Tirol needs to be cleansed of all these intruders."

We all nod in agreement and send the priest on his way with a bag full of food.

"Come quick!" cries Gertrud. It is a beautiful day in late May, I am up to my elbows in the dirt, planting salad, beets, carrots and onions. I hardly look up, but then I see my dear sister waving with both arms as if she wants to fly.

With a sigh, I get to my feet—my back and knees are not what they used to be—and wipe the worst muck off my hands.

"What is it?" I ask when I reach her, but Gertrud is already rushing uphill.

"You will want to see this," she says over her shoulder.

I follow more slowly. If I am honest, I am rather tired of surprises and would much rather remain alone in my garden these days. Our abbey is all about community, but a part of me always thinks that I do not deserve to be here. Not with what happened.

Gertrud is already in the courtyard and so are Juliana and Benedikta. A dozen or so men in Tirolean dress surround them.

But Gertrud only focuses on one man. "Here she is," I hear her say.

"Pleased to make your acquaintance." The man takes off his black felt hat and makes a sweeping bow which makes me want to laugh.

"Magda, meet Andreas Hofer. He is on his way to Bolzano."

I stare at the mystical figure I have heard so much about. He is neither very tall nor good-looking, but even I feel the aura of power. Like most men, he wears a beard, his is blackish and bushy. But it is the eyes that draw me in. His gaze is sharp and intense as he studies me.

"I heard about you, Sister," he says. "Is it true you dressed in a French uniform?"

I nod. I would much rather not think about that endless walk across the mountains. Any one of Tirol's sharpshooters could have picked me off, not learning of his mistake until it was too late.

A twinkle appears in Hofer's eyes. "Most unusual, brave for sure." He looks around. "I understand why you want to protect your abbey."

"We are honored to have you, Herr Hofer," Juliana says. "How can we be of service to you and your men?"

I look past Hofer, suddenly worried about another invasion of hundreds or thousands of men. We are to be hospitable at all times, but the old wounds still ache.

"Just a bit of food and drink will do." Hofer's gaze travels to his men. "Most of our troops are heading south as we speak. I just felt a need to meet you, see the abbey."

I know he means me, but my nun's habit seems to confuse him somewhat. Maybe he expected me to wear pants and a hat. I must have smirked because Juliana throws me a questioning glance.

"Please follow us to the kitchen, Herr Hofer," I say aloud. "We are so pleased you stopped by." In a different world, I might have sat down with him to ask him about his plans and life. Being on the move constantly must be extremely difficult. Just hiking to Bolzano was enough for me. Hofer is younger, around forty, but never sleeping in one place more than a night or two, constantly fighting, constantly being the leader has to be draining.

As it is, we sit down and watch Hofer and his men eat a hasty meal of vegetable soup and meat-filled pie. Within the hour, the men leave, their bags filled with bread, cheese and our best wine.

CHAPTER TWENTY-TWO

August 1809

Below us, all through Tirol, the rebellion surges. There have been several large battles, but thankfully none have been close. Not a single visitor has been here since Hofer's surprise visit. It is as if the country is holding its breath, as if all of us are directing our thoughts toward Hofer's fight to rid the country of Bavarian and French troops.

From up here, it is impossible to say how successful the men are. Determination is one thing, but the enemy is powerful, and commands sheer endless numbers of men. All our soldiers have going for them are their skills of shooting and the knowledge of the land. It may not be enough.

I scold myself for wishing bad things to the Bavarians, all those intruders. And a small voice in my head keeps saying that all I want is to be left alone, for Sabiona to be left alone. It is selfish to say the least. Out there, men perish every day. And all I think about is our little world, close to heaven. I vouch to pray longer and harder to unravel my sinful thoughts and direct them toward the good of our country.

It is a hot day and for once I am not in the mood to be in the garden. On such days, it is best to remain indoors, but my body demands movement.

I leave Gertrud and Benedikta, who are fixing soup for

dinner, and head outside. I should water the two- by three-foot patch of garden I have kept since the birth of my child. Even after Abbess Mayrin told me that she is alive, I could not stop caring for the few flowers, the little rosebush. The flowers wilt quickly in this heat, so I head to the well. It is arduous work to operate the crank and haul water, but the cool trickling sounds calm me.

As I pass through the courtyard, a movement near the tunnel makes me whirl around. My gut tells me that somebody is hiding there, and in that instant, I'm afraid again. Another invasion is happening, the French are back.

I take a deep breath, scold myself. Idiot, it is likely a bird or some other scared creature that has lost its way in the tunnel.

I step closer, shield my eyes from the sun. Only when I am six feet from the entrance do I notice a shadow lurking. "Hello?"

Nothing happens, but I recognize the shape. It is definitely a person. I should run for help, but instead I take another step, then another… into the gloom.

"Sister Magdalena?"

I know that voice, but before I can utter a word, the figure hurries up to me. "Thank goodness it is you," says Andreas Hofer. Even in the gloom, I notice he is in a bad state.

"What happened?"

"I… was outlawed, they are looking for me. I want to shelter for a bit. Do you think—"

"Of course, be quick, before the other sisters see you. We shall go to the guesthouse." I turn on my heels and rush through the courtyard, hoping that nobody looks out of the window. "It has been empty for months. You will be safe."

As we enter the kitchen, where the door has long been repaired, Andreas Hofer sags onto a bench. He looks tired and dispirited and dirty.

"I will bring you water, soap and a towel, food, of course. Tell me what else you need."

Hofer squints and produces what I suppose is a smile.

"Thank you, Magdalena, that is more than I hoped for."

I revisit the guesthouse two hours later, where I find Hofer stretched out on the floor. He has washed, but the state of his dress is hardly improved. He must have heard me, because he clambers up from the ground and retakes his seat on the bench—likely the months in the field have sharpened his senses.

"I can wash your clothes," I say as I sit down across from him.

Hofer ignores my comment, his gaze intense. "Listen, Sister, I do not wish to inconvenience you, or worse, put you in danger. I would never forgive myself."

I scoff, then smile at him. After Franz, who escaped by a hair, not much worries me.

"Do not fret, Herr Hofer."

"Please call me Andreas."

"Nobody will bother you here, Andreas. Just stay inside and rest up. The first cell on the right is made up. You can sleep there in peace. Tonight, I will bring you more food."

Hofer rubs his palms together as if in prayer, throws me a thankful glance before he rises and disappears in the hallway.

When I visit him that evening, I have smuggled bread and a clay pot of soup inside an empty water pail. He sits in the kitchen again.

I watch as he wolfs down his food, then sits back and studies me. "You are a curious one, Sister Magdalena. Father Joachim spoke about you. He is much impressed with your conviction."

"We enjoy Father Joachim's company."

"I do wish to speak with him if possible. Do you think you could send a note to his monastery in Klausen?"

"Of course. Let me find paper and pen, I shall be back soon."

Four days later, Sister Benedikta finds me in the cellar, announcing that Father Joachim demands to see me.

"Could you show him the way here?"

"Of course."

Father Joachim looks in a hurry but bows respectfully. "I came as quickly as possible. What is the matter? Time is pressing. The enemy never sleeps, our men… everybody is tired, ammunition is running low."

"Let us visit the guesthouse," I whisper.

"I would rather—"

I wordlessly hurry ahead, even if Father Joachim thinks me rude. Only after I open the door to the guesthouse and usher the priest inside do I speak. "I am sorry, nobody knows."

"What?"

That is when Andreas Hofer comes hurrying in from the hall. "Joachim, at last."

The priest looks at him open-mouthed, then at me. "Now I understand."

"We had to be careful," I say. "In case the note was opened."

"So that is where you have been hiding." A tight grin runs across Father Joachim's face but disappears at once. "We must fight again, Andreas. Soon, after the truce in Znaim, Napoleon's army is taking over Tirol once more. The people are antsy, our men furious, without you, we cannot possibly win."

Hofer sits down and waves the priest to do the same. "There is money on my head."

"This is larger than you. If we do not defeat them soon, it will have been for nothing."

Hofer nods slowly. "What are you thinking?"

I have heard enough and tiptoe to the door, all the while praying that the French will stay away. Sabiona cannot possibly bear another occupation.

That evening, after I have provided the men with a solid meal of vegetable stew and bread, both disappear, not without thanking me and vowing to return for a visit.

CHAPTER TWENTY-THREE

Fall 1809

I am working the fall garden, planting lettuce and onions. We have harvested apples, pears and plums, which have been canned and dried. I kneel next to the little patch of dirt, my hands in my lap, my face turned to the sun. I have weeded the soil, cut away the rose's dried branches and spent blooms.

Abbess Mayrin is right. It is fine to mourn my child, even if that sadness lets the pain in my chest flare. I must rejoice, she is alive after all, a woman of thirty-five, alive because of me, likely a mother herself.

Keeping her had not been an option… my daughter, who I had named Hilde after my favorite healer, Hildegard von Bingen. I could not have stayed at the abbey, would have been forced to find a roof over my head and work, likely land on the street, a single mother with a child. Good luck. My scoff turns into a sigh.

In the end, losing Hilde was my price to pay to remain at Sabiona, a price no woman should have to pay. Somehow God had chosen for me. Either the child or the abbey.

Suddenly, I feel angry, so red hot angry, I straighten and take deep breaths to force air through my lungs. Why had Mother Mayrin left me thinking that Hilde had died? It was cruel. The ground blurs as I sniff away the tears. Fresh pain joins the old, disappointment about the old Abbess who I considered my mother.

You must forgive, my mind whispers. *She had her reasons.*

It is a beautiful day with sharp colors and the smoky aroma of fall leaves. Juliana has taken over directing the abbey, though I do not feel much closeness for her. She is strict, a fact I do not mind, but her being is all hard and full of edges. I miss Abbess Mayrin's softness. She is mostly in bed now and I am afraid she will not see spring.

On a whim, I decide to visit. The Abbess has lost so much weight, her body consists of nothing but wrinkles and bones. She is asleep, so I sit next to her and study her features. Not much is left of the strong, confident Abbess I met so many years ago. I was a scared girl then, afraid of the men I had left behind, afraid to be found out. At the time, I neither knew I was pregnant nor that Georg had survived.

The first weeks were difficult, the strict schedules, the prayers at night, the silence of my cell. At the time, I thought about leaving one day, maybe letting things settle for a while. Until I found myself pregnant. After I told Abbess Mayrin, she had remained silent for several minutes and then instructed me to keep quiet.

"Child, Magdalena, is that you?" Abbess Mayrin's pale eyes focus on me.

"Mother, it is."

"You have not visited in a while."

I say nothing, well aware that I have stayed away from the Abbess since she told me about Hilde.

"Why did you let me believe that my baby had died?"

Abbess Mayrin just looks at me. For a moment, I am unsure if she even understood my question.

"That was a long time ago."

"The birth, yes, but Hilde would be, what? In her thirties?"

"You are upset."

"You let me mourn her. I would have found peace, knowing of her existence."

"I had to protect the abbey, keep the secret."

"Some secrets are too large to keep." I look at the old woman. "You punished me for my sin."

"Not punish… make it easier."

"For whom? Did you think I might leave and bring shame to the abbey, to our faith?" Had she kept me in the dark because she thought it would be easier for me never to wonder where my daughter had gone, what had become of her? Or was it that she did not want my sin to surface, wanted it hidden and secret? After all, nuns do not get pregnant, do not have children. They are married to God alone.

The Abbess struggles to sit. "I am not without fault, child. I am sorry, I know that now. Our faith is not about stones and buildings, Sabiona only has meaning as long as there are people, loving and devout people." She sinks back on her pillow. "I did you wrong. Please forgive me."

I sink to my knees and place my head on her chest, lie there and listen to the Abbess's labored breathing. She is sleeping again.

Word has reached us that Andreas Hofer won the battle in August, but it was not enough. In a peace agreement, the Austrian emperor Franz I has agreed to give Napoleon, among other things, Tirol. Once again, we are under French rule. All that fighting and struggling, Hofer's and Father Joachim's dedication, has been too little. Power is poison. Those important men, Napoleon and the Austrian emperor, move people around like they are playing chess. We are nothing to them, not human beings with hearts and families and livelihoods. Just something to dispose of as they reside in their palaces.

I pray for the people who have encountered so much bloodshed and deprivation. *Please God, let them be strong enough to endure.*

My thoughts are turning toward the mess of pumpkins piled near the path. I will instruct Gertrud and Benedikta, our younger sister, to make soup and stew. Our numbers have slowly grown over the summer, maybe because so many are tired of the struggle and are searching for a peaceful life. We even had a few pilgrims find their way to us this fall. Each of them is welcome and reminds me of a time when it was normal to share Sabiona with the less fortunate or those who wanted to be closer to God.

I admit there was a time when I believed that God had forsaken us… me. But there was always Mary, mother of God, and the hope in the back of my mind that she would come through.

When I finally straighten, my lower back throbs. I must prepare another salve for winter. All summer, I have collected rose petals which I will mix with olive oil—Hildegard von Bingen's remedy for sore, stiff muscles. Her books are the only thing I never leave behind.

In December, I am awakened by shouts. Sabiona has disappeared under a layer of white, the ground is frozen hard. I pull on my habit, attach coif and veil and as I rush from the room, I almost smash into Benedikta. She looks positively rattled, her cheeks flushed and her eyes wide.

I throw her what I hope is a calming glance and run down the stairs toward the gate. I blink and blink again, but the horrible image remains. Men in French uniforms are marching toward us. I feel Benedikta tremble next to me, but I stand my ground, hoping to show a disapproving expression. Strangely, I am not afraid, just fuming mad.

How many times do we have to lose Sabiona to the enemy? How many times will they soil our holy space and trample on everything we hold dear? I think of our newly scrubbed rooms, the spotless corridors, our stocked kitchen.

"What is the meaning of this?" I shout as soon as the first two men reach us.

They just stare and wave their rifles. Bayonets shimmer in the morning sun. I am all cold inside, not just from the icy wind, but from the ever-growing masses of men spilling into the abbey.

Juliana joins us. "Who are these men?"

"Looks like Napoleon's soldiers again," I say. My throat is dry and hurts, tears press, the feeling of helplessness is back.

A man on horseback approaches. He is short, his hairline receding, curly ringlets frame his cheeks. He stops his horse but remains in the saddle.

"Mesdames," he calls out. "I am General d'Hilliers. We are confiscating your abbey to repurpose it as a fortress." Next to him, two officers watch with swords at the ready as if they are ready to skewer us.

Juliana, next to me, huffs. "Excuse me, General, this is a Benedictine abbey. Sabiona is not equipped to house so many men."

A small smile plays on the general's face. "We will make do, *merci*. You and your sisters must leave. It is easier for all of us."

Easier for you, I want to scream. Despite the freezing air, my head is so hot, it wants to fly away.

"We will discuss it," Juliana says. She takes me by the elbow and guides me inside the main house where men are running to and fro. Somewhere in the distance, I hear a scream. Then another. The men have found my fellow sisters.

"We must go to the guesthouse," I say quietly. "It is the best place to stay."

Juliana nods grimly and I admire her for her composure. "Fetch Gertrud and one of the other sisters to assist Mother Mayrin. I will clear the office."

I remember the kitchen and my cellar, which is barely full again. After finding Gertrud, I rush around to secure some of the food, hide a new vintage of wine from the village behind a wooden panel.

The war is back at Sabiona and I must somehow continue living.

"Have you seen Benedikta?" Gertrud stands in the entrance to my room in the guesthouse. All of us have moved here once more in a matter of an hour.

"Not since this morning, when the French arrived."

Gertrud bites her lower lip. "I am worried about her, she scares easily." She shakes her head. "All those men again."

I try for a smile, though I expect it looks more like a grimace. "We have seen and done it before. We will prevail again."

With a sigh, Gertrud sinks on my bed. "I wish I were as confident as you. How do you do it, Magda? I mean, you have fought so hard for so many years." She wipes away a tear. "I just want to lie down and forget everything."

I resolutely stand up, even though I feel just like Gertrud. I want to crawl into a deep dark hole. All the work we have put forth is lost once more. Our abbey is being eviscerated as we speak. I look to the ceiling, send a silent prayer to Mary. *Please make me strong and allow me to continue, let me help my younger sisters weather this new French storm. Please, I beg you, send the French on their way, let this endless war end.* "We cannot," I say aloud. "We have done it before. They will leave again, it is just a matter of time."

Gertrud jumps back up and grips my hands. "How can you be so confident? They want us to leave, I am sure of it."

"Yes, they do. But that does not mean we will follow their wishes."

Gertrud sets her jaw, wipes away a tear. "Right. I will look for Benedikta now. Let them whistle at me."

This time I smile. "Good girl."

At *Vespers*, our evening prayer, Benedikta is still absent. Gertrud's chin trembles as she moves next to me. "I looked everywhere, it is as if she has vanished. You do not suppose she would have run away?"

I pat Gertrud's hand, hope to infuse some calm into her. "I will help search for her." I am worried myself. Benedikta is so young and sensitive, she reminds me of a young bird.

At dinner, when she still has not appeared, I address

the group. "Our sister, Benedikta, is missing. When have you last seen her today?"

A low mumble rises, heads shake.

"This morning near the main house. Shortly after the soldiers arrived," Gertrud says.

"Did anyone see her talk to the French?" In my mind, I see the young novice, Sister Dorothea, lying on top of Abbess Mayrin's desk, her thighs soiled with blood, her eyes empty. Mother took her away a long time ago, and by the time she returned, she had recovered somewhat. I say somewhat because the former rebellious streak has left Dorothea. She reminds me of a marionette who follows all the rules but whose heart is made of wood.

What if Benedikta fell prey to those men? Many are hungry for a woman. You can see it in their eyes when a young sister passes them. I remember it clearly too. A shiver runs through me. "We should search for her," I hear myself say. "Let's take all the lanterns we can find. I will speak with Commandant d'Hilliers."

Juliana agrees to stay behind, in case Benedikta reappears.

Again, I walk the grounds past lurking French soldiers. *Please let her be all right*, I pray. Here and there, fires burn. The evening is cold, frost crunches beneath my feet.

"I must speak with the general," I announce to the men guarding the entry to the main house.

"He is busy." The boy who has spoken cannot be older than eighteen.

I want to slap him for his arrogance. "It is urgent." I glare at him with all the strength I have.

A bit of doubt has crept into the boy's expression. His fellow guard says something in French I do not understand. At last, the boy turns on his heels and marches away.

Moments later, I am led through the halls of our abbey. The smell has returned. The smell of unwashed skin, urine and worse. I swallow hard as I enter the main office. Juliana had everything sorted neatly. Now it looks like a storm has raged.

Papers are everywhere, books cover the ground.

General d'Hilliers sits behind our desk, impatiently drumming his fingers on the surface. "*Oui?*"

"Sir, one of our sisters is missing."

D'Hilliers looks at me quizzically. "Maybe she went to the village? Is meeting her beau, non?"

I want to yell at him about his ignorance, but discipline wins. "Nuns do not walk off or meet boyfriends, we *live up here.*"

"I have more important things to—"

"We have had incidents before, with French men. One of our sisters was ravished, she never recovered." I cannot keep the fury from my voice. "I would be thankful if you could have at least a small measure of decency. We are married to God, not… loose women."

D'Hilliers straightens in his seat. Maybe I have struck a nerve. "I will organize a search party. What does she look like?"

I give her description as best I can and turn to leave.

"And Sister," the general calls after me. "As I already mentioned, it would be best if you all left. It is safer for you."

With a grunt and a nod, I leave the room. He is probably right, at least the younger nuns should leave. I must speak with Juliana.

Outside, I run into Gertrud, who is on her way to the Church of the Holy Cross. It perches at the highest point and since it still is my favorite refuge, I accompany her.

"Benedikta?" Gertrud calls as soon as we enter.

Nothing.

"Benedikta, are you here?" I cry. "Please come out. It is safe, we will help you."

The church remains silent. Ahead, the sculpture of Mary calls to me. I sink to my knees… *please, holy mother, please show me the way. What happened to Benedikta?*

Gertrud's habit rustles behind me. She sobs quietly.

In that moment, I know something dreadful has happened. The air is cold and still and should calm me, but all

I feel is terror.

I grip Gertrud's hand and together we rush back to Juliana, who is pacing in the kitchen. I report about my meeting with the general and our search of the church.

The sisters are returning one by one, but there is no sign of Benedikta. I fix fennel and chamomile tea to help soothe our nerves.

In my dream, Dorothea appears in my room, shouting at me, wagging a finger, her face morphing into Benedikta's. I awake bathed in sweat.

Somewhere I hear knocking. I throw over my moth-eaten frock and rush into the hall. Again, the sound. Somebody is pounding at the door.

In the first light of dawn, I recognize the boy, one of d'Hilliers's guards, who frowns at me. Obviously, he has not slept and is in a bad mood, because he barks, "Please come at once."

I nod. "I need a few minutes."

I rush back inside, knock on Juliana's and Gertrud's door. Minutes later, we follow the boy uphill. To my surprise, we do not enter the main house, but hurry past it toward the Church of the Holy Cross. Straight past it leads a path to the outer edge of the abbey. Below is nothing but sheer rock, below that the Eisack valley.

By the wall, three soldiers wait, their expressions hard to read. General d'Hilliers steps from the shadows. "I am afraid we have bad news." He swallows. "Your sister… she must have jumped or fallen…"

He points at the wall… beyond.

"No!" Gertrud cries.

I take her hand and together we walk to the wall, lean forward over the edge. Maybe fifty feet below lies Benedikta on an outcropping of rock. Her habit ripples in the icy wind. I feel nothing, not the cold or the rushing air, all I see is Benedikta's still face. It is as white as her wimple. She is dead.

In that moment, two more soldiers appear with ropes

they attach to the wall, climb across and disappear.

One of them yells something, then the other.

D'Hilliers rushes over to us. We have been standing together, holding hands, praying. Gertrud is sobbing while Juliana and I are trying to hold it together. "She is alive."

Gertrud tears lose and runs to the wall, I follow. The men are being pulled up now, one of them is carrying Benedikta over his shoulder.

One of the soldiers has produced a horse blanket on which we place our young sister. Her eyes are closed, but indeed a slight wheeze rises from her throat.

I drop to my knees, carefully take Benedikta's hand. The knuckles are scraped up and bloody. That little movement elicits a moan. "Dearest child, what happened? We are here now."

"Let us bring her to your quarters. I will call my doctor." D'Hilliers nods briefly and marches off.

I just look at the young novice, the little red cross on her wimple, the smooth skin on her cheeks. Even without a doctor or lifting her habit, I know she is broken and closer to God than here to us. Gertrud kneels next to her across from me, tears streaming.

"Why did you do that?" she whispers. "There's always a way, a solution."

I stare at Gertrud. What is she talking about?

Benedicta opens her eyes, apparently tries to focus. She mumbles something, then smiles at Gertrud and is gone.

I close the girl's staring eyes as Gertrud cries. Snowflakes dance and land gently on Benedikta's habit, white dots like feathers. I pray silently, ask God to welcome her. I cannot remember a time when we lost a young sister. Usually, we grow old here, a slow and gradual death that makes us thankful to go. I think of Abbess Mayrin, who is lying in her room on the verge. She does not even know the French are back. It is better that way.

CHAPTER TWENTY-FOUR

Benedikta is buried in our cemetery. It is Christmas and the usual joy of celebrating our Lord's birth remains absent.

Though Tirol's rebellion has been squashed, the French soldiers seem antsy and stay out of our way. Not that we come near them much. I have been trying to speak with Gertrud, find out what could've made Benedikta jump to her death. But Gertrud hardly speaks and if she isn't working, spends much time praying.

The guesthouse is closing in on me, so I take a walk across the grounds. Snow softens my step, swirls across my face. Near the gate, a clump of French are leading six Tiroleans, their hands bound tightly behind their backs, toward one of the buildings, that apparently functions as a prison. The young men are rebel fighters. Hardly older than eighteen, they look exhausted and terribly cold.

I follow slowly, sort of wander, hoping not to raise suspicion. Indeed, they are taken to an abandoned cellar beneath the main house. A long time ago, we kept wine kegs there, but there hasn't been any time to care for the little vineyard down the hill, nor do we have funds to buy new kegs.

Our coffers are as empty as they have ever been, but what does it matter?

Ahead of me, doors crash closed. The French return,

talking among themselves, some laugh. What a joke it must be to incarcerate mere boys. The old anger rises as I hurry into the corridor, then down the stairs. There is no light down here, just gloomy, icy air.

I slip silently around the corner and let out a breath. Nobody is around. That is, out here. Beyond the iron doors, I sense movement. Also, my nose tells me that there are men down here.

I tiptoe to the door, peek through the little window. "Hello?"

On the other side, somebody moves. "Yes?"

"It is Sister Magdalena. How many are in there?"

"Near fifteen, sister." The voice is young and fearful. "It is terribly cold, we have no food, hardly any water, no blankets."

"Let me see what I can find. I will return."

"Thank you, sister."

In the guesthouse, I take stock of our provisions. Having learned from previous occupations, I have hidden some of the preserves, the dried vegetables, flour and potatoes. Winter has barely begun and we have no access to additional sustenance. But doesn't God provide? Doesn't he always show us a way? Some way. These young men won't live long if we do not help.

When Gertrud enters with a bit of greenery to decorate our table, I take her aside. Her cheeks are damp with tears, the skin around her eyes puffy.

"I need your help," I whisper. "The French have caught some of our local fighters." I tell her about the cellar now turned prison. "I want to help them. We need to bring them food, collect blankets."

Gertrud shakes her head. "I doubt the French want us to help their prisoners."

"We will find a way."

Again, Gertrud shakes her head. She turns to busy herself at the wood stove, when I catch her arm. "What is going on? Your heart is heavy, maybe I can listen."

Gertrud tears loose, turns her back to me.

I step next to her, watch her face where fresh tears glitter. Wordlessly, I wrap an arm around her, pull her into an embrace. So we stand as Gertrud sobs against my shoulder.

"It is all my fault," she says after a while between hiccups. "Benedikta is dead because of me."

I take her shoulders, look at her. "What happened?"

Gertrud swallows a couple of times, then lowers her head. "She came to me this summer, shortly after she arrived. Told me that she was in love and that her parents had sent her here to *forget* about the man. They said he was unsuitable, too poor to marry. Benedikta would not hear of it. She wanted to leave, especially after the letter."

"What letter?"

"Her beloved wrote to her, said he would run away with her, take her to Italy. They were going to meet in Bolzano." Gertrud finally looks at me. "I told her it was too dangerous with the people's uprising. You went down there, with all those men on the roads, the constant battles, the snow. I told her to wait until spring, though, I…"

"What happened?"

"She wrote to him that she would meet him after the winter, like I suggested. And then she received another letter, this time from her sister."

I want to shake Gertrud to come to the point, at the same wondering how all this correspondence was smuggled past us, *and* the French.

"Benedikta's beloved had decided to join Andreas Hofer's sharpshooters to pass the time and help rid us of the French. He was killed on November 1 at the last battle of Bergisel." Gertrud sinks onto a chair. "If I had not told her to wait, she might be in Italy by now, happy and in love instead of… cold in the ground—like him."

I take Gertrud's hand, squeeze her fingers. "It is no more your fault than the new French occupation. She likely would have died of exposure or ravaged by soldiers." I gently lift her chin, so she looks at me. "I would have done the exact same thing, recommended to wait until the weather broke."

Gertrud jumps from her chair and throws herself at my chest. "Oh, Magda, why did I not come to you, tell you about her troubles? I just thought it was better to keep her secret. Will you forgive me?"

"Oh, child, what nonsense. There is nothing to forgive. You wanted to help your fellow sister out of love and benevolence. If anything, you need to forgive yourself. Benedikta is with God and so is her beloved."

We hug a final time before Gertrud wipes her face and produces a weak grin. "You said you need help?"

CHAPTER TWENTY-FIVE

Several times now we have managed to smuggle food and blankets to the men in the cellar. I did confide in Juliana, who went to see the general, asked him to allow us to help the prisoners. But he declined, said his men had hardly enough and that there was a war on. Really?

So we have resorted to other methods. My thoughts return to one-eyed Franz who I saved from certain death, helping him escape and who in turn saved my life when I was about to be executed. He must be a grown man now, maybe has a family. I hope. So many people have lost their lives in the many years of war, if not in battle, then from injuries and disease and starvation.

Gertrud is up early, baking bread. She has been making twice the amount, enough to take extras to the cellar. I worry about running out way before spring, I worry more about the men dying in that dark, dank and freezing space. It is the end of January and at night, temperatures fall well below freezing.

After high mass, I rush back to the kitchen, Gertrud in tow. We have already packed bread in a bag which I can bind around my waist and hide beneath the habit. Gertrud rushes to the cellar ahead of me to make sure there are no guards. The French do not seem to think there is much risk of the men escaping. The iron door is solid, so are the four-foot walls. But they do go down there to provide water and on occasion exchange latrine buckets.

Gertrud appears and nods that the way is clear. I follow her into the semi-darkness. Through the iron rods, I make out a huddle of men. As soon as they see us, they hurry to the door.

"Bless you, sister… thank you… you are so kind," they say as we stuff bread loaves through the opening. The men smell like death, their clothes appear so soiled, they have lost their color.

Outside, voices can be heard. I freeze, listen.

Gertrud tugs at my sleeve. "Quick, we must go."

Just three more loaves. I push them into the shaking hands of the men, when I hear footsteps approach on the steps. *Please, God!*

There is no place to hide down here, so we walk quickly toward the staircase. Too late. Six French soldiers are heading down, then stop when they see us.

I bow my head, intent on passing by them. At first, that seems to work, but then one of them says something in French. Two of them take hold of our arms and pull us upward into the light.

We march in silence toward the main house, up the stairs to the general's office.

"What is the meaning of this?" We are obviously interrupting General D'Hilliers's breakfast, because in front of him lie the remains of some kind of hard cheese, bread and red wine. He takes another sip before he motions one of the soldiers to clear everything.

At first, Gertrud and I stand quietly, but then I lose my patience. "Sir, General, we brought the men something to eat. You are obviously not interested in keeping them alive, but our faith demands that we help the needy."

I straighten my shoulders and force myself to look at the man who has stolen our home once again.

D'Hilliers squints at me, then throws his napkin on the desk. "Damn you women. These men are prisoners of war and none of your concern." He takes another sip and continues.

"That is precisely why you must leave. Now! I have instructed Bishop Lodron to find other homes for you. Sabiona is perfect as a fortress."

"But sir, we cannot leave. The weather is forbidding and this is our home." *The only home you will ever have.*

"During wartime, we must make difficult decisions. All of us."

You are the ones invading here, I want to say. But I feel Gertrud's hand on my arm. "May we go?" she says calmly.

D'Hilliers nods, but then calls after us. "Do not let me catch you again. I do not want to arrest you, but I will."

"Let him try," I mumble. But then the path blurs in front of me and I am glad Gertrud holds on to me.

"He wants to throw us out," Gertrud announces as soon as we enter the guesthouse. "Has already asked the bishop to find other homes for us."

Everyone begins to speak at once, but Juliana calls for silence. "Let Gertrud and Magdalena speak. What happened?"

"They caught us in the cellar, feeding the prisoners," I say. But then I cannot go on. I just sit there while the exchange with the general and the words *you must leave* echo through my head. How often have they wanted to force us from Sabiona?

"…made us see the general," Gertrud continues. "He was none too pleased and told us that our dear abbey will become a French fortress. Bishop Lodron is supposed to find new homes for us as we speak. Magda told him that the weather was too forbidding to travel. He said we all have to make sacrifices because there is a war on."

"Men!" Out of Juliana's mouth, it sounds like an insult. And it is. All they do is come up with excuses to fight wars, take over lands and people they have no right to. For power and greed. I want to spit, I am so mad.

I am obviously not the only one, because the room erupts in excited and irritated chatter.

Again, Juliana asks for quiet. "Let us wait and see." She turns to me. "For the time being, we must stay away from the prisoners. I am afraid the general may do something drastic."

Too worked up to deal with my wardrobe that is in high need of mending, I head back outside. It is easier to think in peace and quiet, and I head for my favorite Church of the Holy Cross.

But the path is clogged with soldiers and villagers, packing pews, sculptures, scriptures and wall hangings onto horse carts. All the things we were able to recapture last summer are leaving us anew. I am so stunned, I just stand there, open-mouthed.

"Out of the way, Sister. Hurry."

"No, not again," I shout. But I can only watch as the abbey is stripped of everything.

I recognize one of the villagers, a farmer who used to deliver rye and oats. He nods at me, then lowers his gaze. He knows what went on last year, how our things were stolen.

That's when four French pass me, carrying the church's holy cross. How often have I prayed beneath it? Tears burst, but I am beyond caring. I rush forward, want to touch the cross a last time. "You leave me too, Father of Sabiona."

As the French men shout something and push me aside, four locals rush forward to take the cross from them.

The farmer gently pats my arm. "We will take good care of it, Sister. I promise."

But my focus lies on the heart of my church that has been ripped away and is being carried toward the exit. Several more villagers have joined the procession and are walking quietly behind the cross. I run past them, take hold of the ancient wood.

You are strong, you will prevail. The words are so clear, at first, I think somebody has spoken next to me. But the locals just stand there and watch me, their expressions a mixture of regret, sympathy and sadness.

My arm falls away a second time as resolve floods through me.

I will find a way.

CHAPTER TWENTY-SIX

February/March 1810

I am up, washing for *Prime*, fighting the cold. The French have taken the last of our firewood and I do not know how we will make it through the next months. We can neither cook nor bake and the building is nearly as cold as the outside. I shall speak with Juliana and Gertrud about walking to Klausen to ask for firewood or at least get help cutting trees. Some of the younger sisters will have to accompany me.

I consider asking the general for horse and wagon, even though I do not relish the thought of facing him. He is waiting for us to leave. Ever since we got caught in the cellar, feeding the prisoners, he appears at the most unexpected places, has already asked Juliana three times when we will move.

Bishop Lodron has sent a note that we can stay at his summer residence or, of course, rejoin our families.

What families?

I will leave here only if they force me.

My mind on the task of heating our house, I almost do not hear the noise outside. I pull my spare habit over my wool underthings and rush outside.

Gertrud is already in the kitchen, her eyes like blue question marks. She follows me wordlessly, the two of us are like an old couple where one can predict the other's moves.

Men are spilling in through the gate, men in Tirolean attire—our men. What is going on and why aren't the French shooting?

I look for a familiar face, find none and stop the next man. "What is going on?"

He throws me a small grin. "New orders. We are cleaning house—the French are leaving." The grin broadens. "You are getting your abbey back."

My eyes rise to the heavens, thank you, God, for sending us help.

By evening, all the French have gone. General D'Hilliers rode out on his horse, head held high. Once again, we must clean the filth of our occupiers. Thankfully, the younger sisters do most of the manual work, again some of the villagers come to help.

Father Joachim arrives in early March. He has lost weight, his nose curves like a beak in his gaunt face.

"Will you break bread with us, Father?" I ask. "Gertrud has cooked soup."

To my surprise, the priest shakes his head, just sags onto a bench near our fountain. "I will not stay, but I thought you should know…"

"Know what?"

Father Joachim swallows, tears glitter. "Andreas is dead. The French court-martialed him, he was executed last month, in Mantua, Italy."

I say nothing, just sink next to him.

"He was betrayed by a fellow Tirolean, a local, after all he did for us, the country." Father Joachim rubs his red beard where the first silver has appeared.

"How?"

"After that last battle on November 1, Andreas took to the mountains near his home. He had told me he would hide there if things did not work out. Apparently, a neighbor told the French. Andreas was arrested at the end of January."

I grip Father Joachim's hand, squeeze hard to distract

myself from crying. It is not just because Hofer was murdered, but because of the evil that pervades everything. With so much anguish brought by the French and Bavarian occupation, how can a local betray the leader of the Tirolean people? How does God see and allow it?

"He was a hero," I say at last.

Together we sit there, heads low, praying.

After a while, I look up. It is quiet in the courtyard, maybe my sisters sense that the priest and I need solitude. "What about you?"

Father Joachim sighs. "I am in hiding… at Castle Tschengls near Bolzano. I just had to get out for a bit."

"What will you do, I mean, after this is over?"

"I do not know. Maybe I will go to Vienna. It is a large city. One more priest will hardly raise suspicion." He chuckles bitterly. "I hope."

"I will pray for your safety."

"Please tell the others about Andreas," Father Joachim says as he takes his leave. "I do not have the strength right now, please forgive me."

Over the next weeks, sculptures, wall hangings, bibles, miscellaneous books and pews find their way back to us.

On April 15, Palm Sunday, the villagers appear, carrying the ancient cross. It is a long procession of men, women and children, all dressed in their finest. I can only stand there and watch with tears in my eyes as the heart of the Church of the Holy Cross is reinstated. Thank you, Mary!

Gertrud, who has traveled to the village and neighboring towns to organize supplies, reports that no French are to be found anywhere. Has Napoleon really left us alone? Did Andreas Hofer not die in vain after all?

I am weary, cannot trust anymore that we will be left in peace. Too often have we been disappointed.

Gertrud calls me in the evening. "Come quick, Abbess Mayrin," is all she says.

Juliana and two other sisters kneel around the old

woman's bed. I know it as soon as I enter. My old friend is leaving us. I sink to my knees, touch her hand that consists of nothing but bones and skin. "I forgive you, Mother." All I hear is her breathing, no longer smooth and regular, but halting and skipping. Then it stops all together, the room is utterly silent. I gently touch Abbess Mayrin's neck to confirm what I already know.

"Go with God." Straightening, we all hold hands surrounding the bed. The others are praying, but all I can think is that Abbess Mayrin took my secret to her grave. I will be forever thankful to her.

CHAPTER TWENTY-SEVEN

Summer 1814

It has taken another four years, but finally the war is over. Austrian, Prussian, Russian and German armies have defeated Napoleon in March, the treaty of Paris has been signed and Napoleon sent to exile on the island of Elba.

At last, I believe there is hope to permanently rebuild Sabiona. I am nearly fifty-nine years old and my aching bones carry the burden of a lifetime. Though our wood stores have been replenished, our kitchen produces enough food for our sisters, I feel gaunt. We all do.

I am thankful to Juliana for running things and restoring our archives, organizing work details and providing help in the gardens. I still plan our meals, prepare salves and tinctures to treat my sisters. It will take years, if not decades, to recover from the near twenty years of war and occupation.

Still, my heart sings as I make my way to my favorite church. The old cross hangs where it always has and I kneel at its feet. The sun blazes outside, but in here, it is cool and silent.

The door opens behind me, which immediately takes me back to the time when the French intruded. Will I ever find peace and tranquility again? I have to admit to myself that my nerves are weakened if not frayed. It is much harder these days to sink into the calmness of prayer and remain in this state. My ears seem permanently primed to listen for sounds of violent soldiers.

Light footsteps move behind me, then the quiet returns. It must be Gertrud or one of the other sisters praying like me.

But I cannot concentrate, do not find my way into a conversation with God. I rise slowly, my neck complains and my right knee throbs. I must apply olive-rose oil as soon as I return to my room.

"Sister?" The voice is quiet, almost timid.

In the gloom, the woman who has spoken stands in the aisle between the pews. Her dark hair is streaked with the first gray, unlike the young woman next to her, who eyes me curiously.

"May I help you?"

"I... we are looking for Sister Magdalena."

"I am Magdalena." I take a couple more steps toward the two and then stop. I do not know why, no dangerous vibrations come from the visitors. Still, an invisible wall keeps me in place. "What can I do for you?"

But now the woman approaches, the young one in tow. They stop not three feet in front of me, doubt and curiosity written in their expressions. I recognize the similarities between them, they are undoubtedly mother and daughter.

"I must speak to you in private," the woman says. She appears nervous, her gaze darts back and forth and her hands flutter.

I look around, inwardly shake my head. "We can speak here. Only God may listen in."

She chuckles uneasily. "Maybe we can sit? My daughter and I have walked here from Brixen. I am Anna Steiner, and this is my daughter... Maria."

The girl nods at me and immediately lowers her head as if she is too shy to keep eye contact. I say nothing, just point at the last pew for them to sit. The two of them act so oddly, the old impatience rears up inside me. My garden awaits.

Anna clears her throat, then looks at me with new

resolve. "Mother died last week."

"My condolences, child, I will pray for her."

"Thank you, but that is not why I am here. I mean, it is… oh… it is so difficult." She covers her face with both palms and when she lifts them, her eyes glitter.

"Maybe you would like to speak with Sister Juliana, she oversees the abbey." Secretly, I wonder if Anna's daughter is supposed to join us to become a nun. It happens all the time that families bring their daughters to us.

"No, no, it is you we came to see." Anna's gaze rests on my face, wanders over my habit. "As I said, my mother passed last week and, on her deathbed, she told me that she could not have children. She said I was not her real daughter, that your former Abbess came to her with a newborn babe. She did not say where it came from, just asked Mother to raise me."

All of a sudden, I am back in that room, blood pools in Abbess Mayrin's bed as the pain tears through me in waves. I hear the tiny whimper as the Abbess cuts the cord, wraps the baby in old rags and places her in a wicker basket.

"…about it."

"What?" I have not heard a word.

"I said Mother saw the Abbess many years later when the abbey was occupied by the French. Apparently, Mother asked who the babe had come from. I mean, she knew it had to be a nun or some unfortunate young girl. Mother says Abbess Mayrin was feeling weak and tearful about Sabiona, thought all was lost. So, she told Mother about a young sister…"

"Magdalena," I whisper. The room blurs. Until shortly before Abbess Mayrin's death, I believed my baby had died. She had kept me in the dark, afraid my sin would stain the abbey.

But what is sin when it remains concealed, where it can fester and rot, take pieces from the soul until nothing remains? Isn't it better to let it out? To acknowledge and keep it from festering? To learn from it?

What would Benedict say? I have lived chastely, but what happened with Georg cannot be prayed away, worked away or otherwise erased. And why should it? Why should the beautiful life I brought into the world be wrong?

All of a sudden, my knees are too weak to hold me. I sag onto the bench next to Anna.

"Are you all right?" Anna's face is close now, though she does not touch me. I have often thought that a nun's habit is like a harness.

Our eyes meet. "I am just surprised."

"It is a lot, I was unsure whether to come, but I had to know… to see—you." Now Anna's eyes are filled with tears. "You are my real mother, I always felt that something was different at home, but I never expected…"

I look at the woman who is a mother herself. The girl next to her is my grandchild. I have a family. *How sinful*, my mind comments. *You are a nun. How can you have a child?* But how had I been immoral when none of what happened had been my choice? Yet I judge myself and so do others. Abbess Mayrin had, if not judged me personally, considered the judgment of the people. She had hidden my baby from the world, given it another identity. She had hidden it from me, the child's own mother.

But out of all that ugliness, Georg's attack and my horrible escape, something beautiful developed. Seeing this grown woman who appears quite balanced and spiritual, how she interacts with her daughter, watching my granddaughter in her fitted bodice and long woolen skirt, I feel nothing but pride.

If Benedict, if God or Jesus watch me now, how can they condemn my flesh and blood, simply for the mistake of having been born?

"I am very glad you told me." I find Anna's hand, squeeze it. "It must have been very difficult to come here."

Anna nods. Her eyes are as wet as mine. "The tales of your bravery are told everywhere, how you saved the abbey. I could not believe that you are my mother. Your faith must have been stronger than to marry my father."

Georg's lusty grimace appears in my mind and I shudder. "It is true, I did not marry your father, could not. He was… a difficult man. I left my family, not knowing I was pregnant. Abbess Mayrin took me in. An unmarried woman with a child is a grim fate. She convinced me to give it up and I thought… for the longest time, I thought my baby had died."

Anna claps a hand in front of her mouth but remains silent.

"I am so glad you… You must tell me about your life." My gaze wanders to the young woman. "And yours."

The girl watches me curiously, her expression serious.

"Maria is eighteen and engaged."

With those words, the young woman grows animated. "I am to be married at the Cathedral of the Assumption of Mary in Bolzano."

"How exciting." I want to say more, so much more, but how can I even grasp the idea that I now have not only a daughter, but a granddaughter? Me, a Benedictine nun. It is unthinkable in so many ways, a scandal really. Yet, all I feel is joy, a warmth that reaches to my fingertips and toes, engulfs me like a felted wool blanket on a cold winter day.

I think of the day I hiked across mountains in a French uniform to ask a general to spare Sabiona. I had visited the same cathedral, thrown myself on the ground in front of Maria's image, asked for strength and confidence.

Somewhere a bell rings. Time for *None*, our three o'clock prayer. Please, God, I cannot leave my newfound family. Not yet.

The door opens and closes. "Magda, here you are. Did you not hear the bell? Will you come with me?" Gertrud's slight figure comes to a stop next to us. She looks at me and then the visitors. "Oh, I am sorry for disturbing you."

"It is fine," I say smiling. "I will skip prayer and join you later." God must understand that some things require exceptions.

Gertrud stares at me, her mouth opens, then closes. To

her credit, she says nothing, but turns on her heels and hurries off.

I look at the two women, whose faces suddenly blur. I cannot speak, cannot move, just sit there in the presence of my newfound family while tears stream unchecked. As an answer they move closer to me, embrace me one on each side.

"I am so glad you came," I finally croak. "Now tell me more about yourselves."

CHAPTER TWENTY-EIGHT

As soon as I enter the dining room, Gertrud moves to my side. She is good at hiding her thoughts these days, but not good enough to hide them from me. I can tell she is burning to ask me, but Benedict's commandment of silence during meals allows me a short reprieve. In my mind, the encounter with Anna and Maria replays. Anna's eyes are dark like mine, so are Maria's. A smile plays around my lips as I spoon the vegetable soup, take sips of water.

As soon as Juliana gives the signal, I rise. Not fast enough, because Gertrud takes me by the elbow. "Who was that?" she whispers.

Around us, sisters mingle, some on kitchen duty collect our dishes.

"Let us take a walk," I say calmly. Not an hour ago, Anna and Maria left to return to Brixen. I offered them our guest quarters, but they declined. I think they were as overwhelmed about this new truth as I am. Thankfully, it stays light until late and the roads these days should be safe.

Outside, Gertrud reclaims my arm. "I have never seen you like that."

I grin. "Like what?"

"So, so carefree… happy. You are beaming."

"I do not think I ever have either."

Gertrud pulls me to a stop. "Out with it. I cannot stand the suspense."

"You know it is a sin to be impatient or nosy."

"Magda!" Gertrud laughs. "You are impossible."

"All right. Let us sit in the garden and enjoy this glorious evening. It has been an exciting day." In the little garden patch, the one I falsely kept, commemorating the loss of my baby, we sit on a newly installed bench. The sun is still blazing in the west, a black bird sings an evening serenade high on a tree.

All is well and the sky is a dome of cobalt. But even though our buildings, our rooms and community areas have been cleansed, every floorboard scrubbed, every wall wiped down, walkways swept and gardens picked up, something remains like an invisible stain. A visitor would not see it, nobody really can. But to me, there is blood and dirt imprinted on Sabiona. The air is fresh and yet, in the recesses of my mind, I still sense the horrific stench of hundreds of occupiers. But Sabiona carries its history with grace, will serve generations of nuns, pilgrims and visitors as it has served me.

The only thing I can say with conviction is that I believe God made me take this road for a reason. I have spent forty years of my life defending the abbey, survived nineteen years of war to finally realize that life without sin is impossible. My search for perfection has evaded me, it is arrogant to think I can ever achieve it.

But I have made peace with the fact that I am flawed. Why? Because I am human. And though we strive to follow the laws of Benedict, the teachings of Christ, these laws do not define me, only guide me.

I look at my old friend. "I have never told you the reason why I came here. With the help of Abbess Mayrin, I have hidden the truth from others and myself. Let me tell you a story."

We sit in the evening sun until it disappears behind the mountain while I tell Gertrud my innermost secret and explain the presence of the two women.

"You mean you never knew you have a daughter until today?" cries Gertrud.

"As she weakened, Abbess Mayrin told me that the baby was alive. Until then, I had thought…" My gaze falls on the little rosebush, the pink buds. "This was her memorial."

"So that is why you cared for it. Either way, Mother Mayrin should have told you!"

"She meant well," I say quietly. "Though I think burying a secret of this gravity does not work. Something like that has a way of rising to the surface." I take a deep breath. "You know, at first, I was glad. I mean, I thought Hilde had died, and I felt relieved… because of Georg… and… I thought nothing good could come from it. I thought God was punishing me for my sin, that I *deserved* to suffer. Over the years, I grew so sad inside. I kept praying for it to pass, but it never did."

"Maybe you fought so hard for the abbey to forget it all."

I shrug. "Maybe. I always thought it was because I had no place to return to. But it was more than that. Sabiona is my life." I smile at Gertrud. "Though truthfully, had I known the war would last nearly twenty years, I would have long given up. What counts now is that we made it through unscathed." I chuckle. "All right, maybe with scratches and dents, but we are here, still in our abbey close to heaven."

Gertrud nods thoughtfully. "And today you actually met your daughter."

A giggle rises into the evening like the call of a mocking jay. So strange and light, I hardly recognize it as my own.

Gertrud laughs, then puts an arm around my shoulder. "I am so happy you met her. God does work in wondrous ways."

EPILOGUE

I am sitting in the middle of a beautiful garden. White roses grace the tables, garlands move gently between the trees, lights glitter. Around me, people mingle, their speech soft and joyful. All day, strangers have addressed me, thanked me for rescuing Sabiona Abbey.

"Mother, will you not come and join the festivities?" Anna, dressed in a sand-colored linen dress with a moss-green bodice, pulls me from my thoughts.

I smile at her. It is our private joke. Only I know what she means. Everyone else thinks she is addressing a Benedictine nun.

"I am quite content, watching from here." Anna knows I enjoy the solitude and that so many people, even though they are celebrating Maria's wedding, are overwhelming.

Anna places a hand on my shoulder. "How about I tell Maria to sit with you for a minute?"

"No need, child. Let her enjoy her husband, her guests." In the distance, Maria is dancing with her new spouse, her entire being shines with happiness.

Anna smiles, then slides onto the bench next to me. "As you wish."

"Being a part of this, of your lives, is enough. I am an old nun, after all."

Anna turns to me, squeezes my fingers. "You know, at first, I was angry you had given me up. I did not know, did not realize…"

"It is all right, child. We often judge what we do not know. When we have not walked in the other person's shoes."

Anna sighs. "I am glad to have found you. Besides, you are not old, just wise."

I smile at my daughter. My heart is full. In a way, I have been luckier than most. I was able to live my adult life as a nun, follow my convictions and yet… I also know now what it is like to have a child: the intense joy it brings, paired with worry for its wellbeing. Please, God, let her be happy.

We agreed that nobody should know about our relationship. Not even Anna's husband, who I met earlier today, suspects. I am simply a nun, who has been invited to a wedding. Mother Mayrin was right in one thing. It would be scandalous, and many people would not understand, not even Bishop Lodron.

Besides, what does it matter what others think? It is for us to know and cherish. A beautiful person came from something ugly and, in the end, love prevails.

In my heart, I know that Saint Benedict would agree.

AUTHOR'S NOTE

Sabiona Abbey
Founded by nuns from Salzburg, Austria in the 17th century, Sabiona Abbey was a Benedictine cloister on top of the holy Sabiona mountain in South Tirol and what is today northern Italy. From the village of Klausen at the bottom of the mountain, it is a thirty-to-forty-five-minute hike to its gate and four churches. The abbey closed in November 2021 because of a lack of recruits. With its tall, massive buildings and walls, perched at the precipice of the Eisack valley, it is reminiscent of a medieval castle.

Magdalena Told

I came across Magdalena when I visited Sabiona Abbey in 2019. We had hiked the mountain from Klausen and near the abbey's entrance came across a wooden board with a depiction of a nun in a French army uniform.

Next to it was a short description of Magdalena's secret visit to Bolzano, where she begged the French general to save the abbey. My curiosity was awakened, especially after passing through a narrow tunnel into the beautiful abbey, wandering within its walls, visiting the Church of the Holy Cross and admiring the stunning views. It truly feels like one is flying above the earth. After returning from the trip to South Tirol, I began researching Magdalena's life and her upbringing.

Not much is known about her reasons for joining the abbey, only that Mariele Told was the daughter of Anton Told, the innkeeper of the Black Eagle in Niederdorf in the Puster Valley. Born August 22, 1755, she entered the abbey at the age of nineteen and took her vows as a Benedictine nun in 1776. She managed kitchens and cellars for forty-eight years and passed away February 16, 1841.

We can only guess why she left her family and chose to live far from society. Whether she experienced foul play at the pub or had an illegitimate child is unknown and my own creation. It is also unknown whether Magda met Joachim Haspinger, the Capuchin priest. Since Haspinger participated in numerous battles and was stationed at the central cloister in the village of Klausen at the foot of Sabiona Abbey, it is likely that the two knew each other. Whether Andreas Hofer sought refuge at the abbey in August of 1809 is also unknown. To this day, nobody knows where he hid when a bounty was put on his head. It seemed only fitting to have Hofer meet Magda, since both of them were strong individuals who did much for their country.

We do know that Magda refused to leave the abbey, no matter the danger and discomfort of numerous hostile occupations. Her selfless march to Bolzano, asking General Fenner for help, visiting Bishop Lodron in Brixen to ask him to reinstate the abbey, may be the reason why Sabiona Abbey remained in existence for another two hundred years. At the very least, it helped preserve the abbey for her fellow sisters and the people who revered this holy and spiritual place.

Napoleon Bonaparte and the Napoleonic Wars
Napoleon I (1769–1821), French emperor, became a

prominent leader during the French revolution. During the seven coalition wars, Napoleon's troops occupied Sabiona Abbey several times: twice in 1797, in 1805, when France allied with Bavaria and Bavarians occupied the monastery, and 1809/1810. Each time, the foreign occupation did much damage. Even Tiroleans considered Sabiona a valuable spot for a fort and moved in and out several times.

But the largest damage likely happened when, as part of the secularization wave sloshing through Bavaria and Austria, Sabiona lost its identity as a functioning cloister. Bavaria, thanks to Napoleon, in charge of Tirol, had been confiscating the assets of churches and religious orders to fill its coffers. In 1808, it was Sabiona's turn to be stripped of its identity. Not that there was much to be had at this point, as most items of value had long been plundered. For religious institutions and the common folk, who clung to their faith, the damage reached much deeper, though. Religious practices were forbidden, the ringing of church bells banned.

Eventually, as the French reoccupied Sabiona in 1809/1810, Magdalena asked Bishop Lodron in Brixen to rescind Sabiona's secularization. He complied, no doubt with the consent of Bavaria, and well knowing that most earthly wealth had left the abbey.

Hildegard von Bingen

Hildegard von Bingen (1098–1179) or Saint Hildegard was a German Benedictine nun, abbess, poet and scholar of natural medicines. She wrote and published about religion, music, medicine, cosmology and ethics. She is considered Germany's first writing physician and produced two works: *Physica* and *Causae et curae*. Hildegard is mostly known for combining the knowledge of traditional Greek and Latin medical teachings and plants with the teachings of popular medicine and thus making this knowledge accessible for the common person. She also believed that health could only be achieved by keeping body, mind and soul balanced. The Roman Catholic church designated her a saint, other religions also honor her.

Andreas Hofer

To this day, Andreas Hofer (1767–1810) is celebrated as a Tirolean freedom fighter and folk hero. Though not without criticism for some of his actions, he rose to become Tirol's leader and headed the rebellion against the Bavarian and French occupation in 1809. He successfully fought numerous battles with large contingents of Tirolean sharpshooters and, with the support of the Austrian emperor Franz I, briefly moved to the castle of Hofburg in Vienna. He received a medal for his valor, but had to leave when Austria ceded Tirol to Bavaria in the treaty of Schönbrunn (October 1809). After a few more half-hearted attempts at battle and after having been promised amnesty, Hofer moved to the mountains surrounding the Passeier valley near his home, the Sand Inn. In January 1810, Franz Raffl, a neighbor, sold him out for 1,500 guilders. After a court martial in Mantua, Italy, Hofer was executed by firing squad. Supposedly, he refused a blind-fold and told the French "to shoot straight." It is rumored that he cried, "French! Oh, how poorly you shoot!" after he was only injured from the first execution salvo, a final praise referring to the sharpshooting abilities of his men. He is buried in the Hof Church in Innsbruck, Austria.

Joachim Haspinger

Father Joachim Haspinger (1776–1858) was an academic, a Capuchin priest, a troop commandant during the Tirol rebellion and, in his later years, a traveling preacher. He became a priest in 1805 and participated in two major battles with Andreas Hofer. Haspinger, who his men called Father Redbeard, also led Salzburg's men to fight in the rebellion. When French troops squashed the uprising on November 3, 1809, and Hofer lost his last battle, Haspinger fled, first to Castle Tschenglsburg near Bolzano (until October 1810), then to Vienna, where he worked as a priest. He remained interested in politics to his death and is buried next to Andreas Hofer in the Hof Church in Innsbruck, Austria.

Sin
/ sin/
:an offense against religious or moral law
:an action that is or is felt to be highly reprehensible –Merriam-
Webster

In many religions the term *sin* carries the negative connotation of guilt, of wrongdoing, of not living up to the standards of its followers. Committing sins is not only immoral, it is reprehensible.

But what is sinful? When do we commit a sin? Who determines what a sin is or if one has sinned? Does it matter how large or small a sin is?

I found the subject of sin interesting as it also highlights how often we tend to judge others when they behave differently from us or in our eyes transgress from our individual moral framework. I deliberately put my protagonist in situations that may be questionable or downright unacceptable to some. Whenever a religious or political order puts severe restrains or pressures on human beings, or if those human beings are faced with exceptional threats, those humans tend to find ways to circumvent these rules. Sometimes, people's circumstances may require them to disobey, even to commit sins.

I think, we can agree that sin is a complicated term open to much interpretation.

ABOUT THE AUTHOR

Perhaps Annette Oppenlander became a writer of historical novels because she likes to dig in the past. It all started when she asked her parents about their experiences as war children. Over many years, these emotional memories developed into the biographical novel "Surviving the Fatherland." Not only did this story win many awards, it also served as the springboard to a successful writing career.

Ms. Oppenlander likes to shed light on difficult subjects such as World War II from the perspective of civilian Germany, walks alongside ordinary people in the American Civil War or the Middle Ages. To create an authentic historical world, she often uses biographical information, interviews contemporary witnesses and unearths little known facts in the archives.

After studying business administration at the University of Cologne, Germany, Ms. Oppenlander spent 30 years in various parts of the United States. She writes her novels in German and English, and also shares her knowledge – writing workshops, entertaining presentations and author visits to universities and schools, libraries, retirement homes and organizations dedicated to literature – in German and English. She now lives with her American husband and dog Zelda in the beautiful Münsterland in

Germany.

"Nearly every place holds some kind of secret, something that makes history come alive. When we scrutinize people and places closely, history is no longer a date or number, it turns into a story."

From the Author

Thank you for reading 'So Close to Heaven.' My sincere hope is that you derived as much entertainment from reading this story as I enjoyed in researching and creating it. If you have a few moments, please feel free to add your review of the book at your favorite online site for feedback (Amazon, Apple iTunes Store, Goodreads, etc.). Also, if you would like to connect with previous or upcoming books, please visit my website for information and to sign up for e-news:
http://www.annetteoppenlander.com.
Sincerely, Annette

Contact Me

Website: annetteoppenlander.com
Facebook: facebook.com/annetteoppenlanderauthor
Email: hello@annetteoppenlander.com
Instagram: @annette.oppenlander
Twitter: @aoppenlander
Pinterest: @annoppenlander

www.ingramcontent.com/pod-product-compliance
Lightning Source LLC
LaVergne TN
LVHW011009200726
843509LV00011B/1025